W9-BUR-586

A SUNBURNED PRAYER

MARC TALBERT

SIMON & SCHUSTER
BOOKS FOR YOUNG READERS

Simon & Schuster Books for Young Readers
An imprint of Simon & Schuster Children's Publishing Division
1230 Avenue of the Americas
New York, NY 10020

Designed by Anahid Hamparian.
The text of this book is set in 12-point Candida.

Manufactured in the United States of America.
10 9 8 7 6 5 4 3 2 1
Library of Congress Cataloging-in-Publication Data
Talbert, Marc
      A sunburned prayer / Marc Talbert.
           p.   cm.
      Summary: As he makes a seventeen-mile pilgrimage to the Santuario
de Chimayó that he hopes will save his beloved grandmother from cancer,
eleven-year-old Eloy is joined by a friendly dog that helps him keep going.
      [1. Grandmothers—Fiction.   2. Catholics—Fiction. 3. Mexican
Americans—Fiction. 4. Dogs—Fiction.] I. Title.
PZ7.T1415Su   1995   [Fic]—dc20   94-38682   ISBN: 0-689-80125-4

**FOR
JAMES RUGGLES THORPE, JR.**

*up ahead and out of sight
but not forgotten*

WEDNESDAY
OF
HOLY WEEK

"IF I CAN'T TRUST my own mother to keep a promise, who can I trust?"

Eloy sounded so much like his older brother, Benito, he wanted to spit in his own face. But he couldn't do that any more than he could stop shouting.

"You promised! How can you break a promise?"

Eloy could hardly believe what was coming out of his mouth. Shouting was something his brother was really good at, unlike Eloy, who was an expert at whining. But the hot words kept coming. "It was your idea in the first place. How could you do this to me?"

"I know I promised." His mother looked and sounded more tired than angry. "I planned to walk with you on Good Friday . . . you know that. But while you were in school today I got a call from Mrs. Danskin and she needs my help getting ready for a party. Can you believe it? A party on Good Friday! And her house needs a week to get clean, not two days."

"I'll go without you." Eloy glared at his mother. Just then his father came into the kitchen, still smelling of work even without his shirt on. He glanced at Eloy and his mother, looking bored as he tried to figure out what was going on. Eloy kept glaring at his mother. With any luck he would get his father to take his side against her

—it wasn't hard to do these days. "I can do it . . . all by myself. Lots of kids at school have done it before. I don't need no baby-sitter."

"Eleven is too young. I don't want you to walk by yourself." His mother's face changed from tired to stern. "I don't think you can make it to Chimayó on your own and I'd worry myself sick about you all day. Look. Walking to Chimayó . . . it's over sixteen miles . . . seventeen miles, at least. I'm sorry. But we'd end up searching for you, searching up and down the highway in the dark like we were spotlighting for deer or something."

Eloy's father sat down at the kitchen table and leaned back in his chair, folding his arms across his chest, the boredom gone, looking almost as interested as when he watched those boxing matches on TV.

The tiredness returned to his mother's face as she reached out to give Eloy a hug. Eloy dodged like a boxer, shrugging her off.

"Please, Eloy." There was pleading in her voice. "What you want to do is good. I'm proud of you for wanting to walk. We all want your *abuela* to get well. I'd do anything . . . *anything* . . . if I thought it would work. But . . . "

"You still want to walk, huh?"

Both Eloy and his mother looked to where Eloy's father sat. Eloy barely nodded, hating himself for hiding his true feelings, for trying not to look eager. That was something else Benito was great at. The less eager Benito looked about something, the more you could bet he wanted it.

"Look, Eloy. Don't be stupid. If God answered our prayers we'd all be rich as Californians." His father unfolded his arms and sat up, with a glare that put to shame anything Eloy could do with his own face. "Listen. Nothing is fair in life, anyway, so grow up and get used to it. Nobody lives forever. And God never answered nobody's prayers that I heard of. Not even Father Ribera's prayers for people to help fix up that church of his. Don't be stupid. It's not a pilgrimage. It's just a long, hot, stupid, miserable walk. It's just a way to get good and sunburned. Walking ain't gonna do nothing . . . for nobody."

"Shut up!" His mother stepped toward his father, making the sign of the cross several times with threatening, karate-like movements. "If you were making more money, I'd call up Mrs. Danskin and tell her to go find somebody else. And then Eloy and I would walk . . . for his *abuela* . . . and for your sins too!"

Eloy stood in front of his arguing parents, hoping that his mother would change her mind to spite his father, or vice versa. But as they argued it became clear that for different reasons both of them agreed he shouldn't walk to Chimayó.

So what, Eloy thought. Let them argue. If he had to, he'd walk and then hitchhike back from Chimayó with that holy dirt before his parents came home from work. They'd never know.

When Eloy turned to leave all this bickering, he was surprised to see Benito standing off to one side of the kitchen door, his eyes half closed, a thin smile on his face. The smile blossomed, mocking him. Eloy threw an elbow at his brother as he walked by, but Benito stepped away just in time.

"Jerk," Eloy muttered as he walked past. It was a dangerous thing to say so, instead of heading to the bedroom he shared with his brother, Eloy retreated to his *abuela*'s bedroom. He told himself he'd wanted to go there anyway.

Her door was open just enough for him to turn sideways and slip in. He sat at the end of her small bed. She looked shrunken, which made the bed appear large. He could hardly believe it was her, the same *abuela* who made ants look lazy. He watched as she mumbled through a rosary, her fingers clinging like insect legs as they crawled over the beads. Her eyes were closed so tightly they seemed to pull the rest of her face into their sockets. Eloy said hello. Twice. But when she was concentrating in this way she didn't seem able to hear the sounds of human voices.

Small sounds were different. Sometimes Eloy wondered if old people, being closer to death, heard things from the other side. The voices of angels? Or devils, perhaps? As he watched his *abuela* a coyote yip-yipped in the distance. Sure enough, at that small sound her eyes and mouth opened. The skin seemed to fall from her face, stopping only at the last possible moment.

"I don't care what they say," he told her. "I'm gonna walk for you on Friday. I'm gonna bring back some of that holy dirt . . . to get rid of the cancer." He moved around on the bed to be close and said it again. "I'm gonna walk for you tomorrow." He wanted to make sure she understood. She closed her mouth, her smile a grimace.

"No, *m'jito*," she whispered, closing her eyes now too. "You don't agree with your papa and momma. But you must learn to obey, to do what they say." Her eyes opened and she looked at him with great sadness. "They're gonna need you to help them when I'm gone."

Eloy pleaded with his eyes. Until the cancer, his *abuela* would have taken charge, told his mother and father they were wrong. They lived in her house and they had always listened to her. But not now. Since the cancer, she no longer took charge. Eloy wished she would this once—for her own sake.

"Thank you all the same," she wheezed. *"Dame un besito."*

How could his *abuela* agree with his parents! Didn't she know how important this was—to her—to him? But he knew it was pointless to argue. He leaned over and kissed her on the cheek, her skin feeling soft as a fresh tortilla, but cold instead of warm.

GOOD FRIDAY

ONE

ELOY OPENED HIS eyes with a jerk and looked into the same darkness he saw with his eyes closed. The pain came again, from the pit of his gut. He blinked but the darkness remained.

A sooty light from the window began to settle on him, letting him see the mound of his own body, naked under the blanket. Another pain came, sharper this time. His whole body twitched and the light on the blanket seemed to fly up and scatter like dust.

"¡Híjole!" he muttered. The sun wasn't quite up yet—it had to be before six o'clock—and it was time to get moving.

Last night, before going to bed, he'd drunk six glasses of water, one right after the other. He'd done that once before on Christmas Eve—four years ago, when he was seven. He'd figured then that he would wake up when he had to go to the bathroom and beat everybody else to the presents, maybe even switch around some tags for fun.

Six glasses of water were almost more than his stomach could hold, but at least this time he'd awakened just before the water came out like it did from the high-pressure wand his brother used to clean his car at the Bubble Heaven in Santa Fe.

Eloy moved slowly, almost afraid to breathe, afraid he might burst. His bladder ached more than it had ever ached before. Why hadn't the pain awakened him sooner? Eloy peeled back his covers and gently sucked in his gut to make room as he sat.

Shivering in the cold air, he swung his legs, feeling for the floor with the soles of his feet. The linoleum next to his bed had bubbled and it made a sound like the bounce of a basketball on gravel whenever he stepped on it. He brushed the bubble's crown with one heel and planted his feet off to the side. To his bare feet the cool linoleum had always felt like the inside of a drying pelt, tacky with blood. He shuddered.

Groping next to his feet, Eloy picked up the clothes he'd stashed there and tiptoed past his older brother's bed. The air smelled faintly of stale cigarette smoke. He saw that Benito was hugging his pillow to his face, his mouth opened and his lips smashed off to one side, as if he were trying to kiss his own ear. His brother's face was relaxed and loose in sleep. It was a softer face than Eloy had seen for awhile, the face of the brother that Eloy used to shadow and pester and beg to play with, before his brother grew tough and silent and hard.

Benito had thrown off his covers in the night and Eloy assumed that, once more, his brother had come home late after partying with his *vatos* and fallen into bed with his clothes on. Eloy smiled. If Benito's jeans get any tighter, he thought, there won't be any room for what makes him a man. Every little thing he's got will tuck tail, crawl inside . . . and my brother will become a girl!

Immediately, Eloy regretted thinking this thought

on Good Friday. It was too early to think straight. But lately his brother had started walking as if he had baseballs packed in his pants instead of *huevos* the size of a hummingbird's. It drove Eloy crazy. For this one profane thought he hoped that God would understand.

Eloy gasped as pain once more shot up from his bladder. If he didn't get outside fast he was going to lose control. He grabbed himself and pinched.

In the hallway, he heard his father's snoring coming from behind, and ahead he saw a sheet of light pushed out from under the door of his *abuela's* bedroom.

Since she came home from the hospital, his *abuelita* was in constant pain. She often kept her light on when she couldn't sleep at night. She said that she'd left the hospital to die in the comfort of her own home. But there was no comfort at home for Eloy's *abuela*.

Walking past her door now, he surprised himself by making the sign of the cross. He held his breath, wondering if she were asleep or giving her beads a workout. Had he made a small sound walking past her bedroom that she might have noticed?

Eloy entered the living room and was just about to break into a trot when he saw his mother sleeping on the couch. Eloy hated himself for trembling as he crept by her. Was she sleeping there because of his father's snoring, which rumbled from the other end of the house, even through the adobe walls? Or had his mother and father fought again during the night? They often did since learning of his *abuela's* cancer, whispering so that *abuelita* wouldn't hear. They didn't fool anybody. Or maybe she had come out onto the couch hoping to catch him if he tried to join the pilgrims as they walked to the Santuario de Chimayó. He'd tried to talk her into it again yesterday. He'd started out nice and reason-able, which didn't work. Neither had whining. So he'd ended up shouting again. Once more she'd forbidden him to go to the Santuario for the holy dirt that people rubbed on themselves or ate to cure diseases—even blindness and deafness, even cancer and depression, or to prevent babies from being born stupid.

To his surprise, Eloy heard his mother's voice from last night in his head. The voice was so clear that he thought at first she might be talking in her sleep, or that maybe she was awake. "You can go, all right, Mister Smarty Pants. You can go . . . *if* you get your brother or your father to walk with you!" She might as well have told him to ask the archbishop for dinner.

Eloy didn't want to remember any more of last night. Once in the kitchen, he rushed to the back door and stumbled onto the packed dirt of the backyard. The cold air caused him to gasp. Dropping his clothes on a scrap of flagstone, he spread his legs a little more with each step, pushing his belly out like his father's. And then, trying not to shiver, thinking of Bubble Heaven, he let fly. He aimed for the black-tinted windows of Benito's falling-apart, low-riding car, which was parked beyond a short stone wall. It was so dirty Eloy would have been doing his brother a favor. He almost hit it.

The stream of water sparkled, making a beautiful wavering arc in the tarnished silvery light, ending just this side of the wall among some flowering daffodils. If he'd walked up to the wall when he finished, Eloy wouldn't have been surprised to see a pile of diamonds where his pee hit. As he watched the water he felt he was letting go of all the fear, anger, and frustration of hearing his mother and father argue again last night.

The tension in his stomach began to melt and he realized how much his *abuela*'s cancer was eating away at him, too, in its own way.

The arc hesitated and grew shorter, retreating until it disappeared altogether. He shook off the last few remaining diamonds and reached for his clothes. They were cold and he shivered as he put them on.

Eloy looked at the mountains, their black outlines now rimmed with a frosty light from the hidden sun. He didn't like what his mother had said last night, or what his father had said two nights ago. Sure. He was going to beg God, the same guy who let his *abuela* get the cancer in the first place, the same guy who could have prevented it by lifting His little finger. Sure, he was going to beg for help from the same guy who let His own son be killed on a cross.

But what choice did he have? Who else could he ask? If God didn't at least listen to people who had problems, then what was the point of even trying to do what was right?

TWO

THE COMING SUNRISE stirred the night air and Eloy wished that he'd stashed a jacket with his other clothes. Hugging himself for warmth, he walked down the flagstone path that went through the packed dirt of his yard. Eloy saw that for the fifth time in so many nights, something had tipped over the garbage can by the kitchen door. Bottles, cans, paper, and assorted junk were scattered around. The lid had rolled toward the *arroyo* that cut between his house and the Jaramillos' mobile home next door.

Everybody in Pedernal had complained about their garbage cans being messed with. At first Pablo Jaramillo, the village *mayordomo*, suggested that it must be raccoons living near the river. This year they were more numerous than ever, and bolder. He suggested that everybody should purposely leave their dogs out at night to chase them away. That hadn't helped, but it gave people a chance to complain about Jesús Anaya's pit bulls and blame them for the problem all along. Of course that made Jesús angry, so two nights ago he agreed to lock up his dogs in the cab of his pickup to prove that his dogs were too good to eat trash. That night the cans were raided again, which would have proved Jesús was right about his dogs not eating garbage except that they ate the upholstery off his truck's bench seat.

Nobody could figure out the mystery of the trash cans. Maybe it was *un espectro* feeling restless with spring coming on and wanting to take a little ghostly stroll from his thawing grave at the *camposanto* by Father Ribera's fallen-down church. Maybe it was something else. In the meantime, everybody in Pedernal more or less picked up their garbage each day.

Picking up his family's garbage had been Eloy's job before catching the school bus. He'd picked it up so often he was becoming very familiar with some of it. If he didn't see one of the embarrassing pieces in plain sight he would hunt for it until he found it. Eloy hated to take time this morning, but he picked up the more obvious pieces anyway before putting the lid on the can. He didn't want his parents to see the garbage, come looking for him to pick it up, and then notice he was gone.

Feeling warmer now, he stopped at the mailbox by the road. The mailbox had long ago lost its door and its shape—it was the target of sticks and rocks. Eloy pulled out the stone that served as the door and then the paper bag he'd stuffed clear to the back last evening. The night air should have kept everything in the bag nice and cold, but even so Eloy smelled the salami and the yellow cheese he'd rolled in a couple of tortillas with a little mayonnaise and a lot of squeezed-out mustard.

A few steps from the mailbox was a forsythia, its flowers so bright yellow in the pre-dawn light they looked fake. From under the bush Eloy pulled two old canteens that were covered with canvas, moist with the dawn and smelling of mildew. Each canteen attached to a woven cloth belt with hooks that fit into grommet holes. They had belonged to his *abuelo,* Esequiel Abeyta, who had fought in World War II. Eloy liked to think that his *abuelo* had used these same canteens when he made his pilgrimage to Chimayó in thanks for surviving the Bataan death march in the Philippines.

His *abuela* often spoke of his *abuelo* making his pilgrimage to the Santuario on Good Friday of 1946. He'd started alone and ended up walking with veterans from Chupadero, Río en Medio, Tesuque, Española, Santa Fe, and other places too. Nobody planned it that way. It had just happened, like a sign from God.

Every year on Good Friday some people walked while carrying wooden crosses made of rough-sawn six-by-sixes, like Christ himself might have carried during the Stations of the Cross, on his way to being crucified. Instead, his *abuelo* had carried a small statue of St. Francis he'd fashioned in the prisoner-of-war camp out of a kind of wood he'd never seen before or after, using anything hard for tools but mainly gouging at it with his thumbnails. Sticking out her chin with pride, Eloy's *abuela* said that the memories this St. Francis held for his *abuelo* had made it far heavier than any large wooden cross.

Something had happened to Esequiel Abeyta during the walk to this place of miraculous dirt—what, Eloy's *abuela* never knew exactly. He could talk about Japanese abuse in the prisoner-of-war camp, but he couldn't talk about his pilgrimage. She said that whenever he tried to tell her what happened, tears would choke off his words and flood his eyes. His hands would shake and his lips would quiver and he would shake his head, as if apologizing for even trying to explain something so powerful and mysterious.

But she had her ideas. "He must have met *Our Lord of Esquípulas . . . el Cristo Negro . . .* on the road to Chimayó," she would say, crossing herself several times. That was quite a thing for his *abuelita* to think— the Santuario had been built to glorify *Our Lord of Esquípulas.* Eloy knew many people who believed he was a saint who made miracles happen for those who visited the old statue of him there and took of the dirt he blessed with his presence.

When his mother announced several weeks ago that she was going to do the pilgrimage to Chimayó, it was remembering this story of his *abuelo* that had inspired Eloy to want to join her. After strapping on the canteens, he checked the pocket of his jeans to make sure he had the rosary his *abuela* gave him for Christmas three years ago. What a disappointing gift it had been at the time. But last night, while he was getting ready, the thought of it had popped into his mind. The rosary had seemed the right thing to take and he'd searched until he found it at the bottom of his sock drawer.

The road was deeply rutted from a winter of snow and ice that froze and thawed repeatedly. Gravel had long since sunk into the mud, never to be seen again. As the gravel disappeared, a thick yellow clay would rise through the mud. Wet, the clay floated like oil and was just as slick. Today the road was dry and the clay felt powdery as Eloy stepped on it.

He kept his eyes on the road, not wanting to twist an ankle at the beginning of his pilgrimage. But he glanced up when he passed the mobile home of his best friend, Felix. Unlike Eloy's house, which was built of adobes, Felix's mobile home had all the newest conveniences and gadgets. It had shag carpeting, built-in closets instead of *trasteros*, and heated air from floor ducts in every room instead of heat from a wood stove in the kitchen. Eloy often wished his family lived in a mobile home.

As he walked by, a puff of wind hit the back of his neck and Eloy felt he was being watched. He stopped and slowly turned around. Maybe it was the garbage-scattering ghost breathing down his neck—or a *brujo*. For the first time he noticed that no dogs were barking at him as he walked down Pedernal's main road. Ordinarily that would have been a great relief—Eloy tormented them every chance he got. They'd grown to hate him as much as he hated them. But now the silence spooked him. He'd been told that dogs never barked at *brujos*, knowing what witches could do to them.

Lucky for Eloy, the sun crested the mountains at that moment, spilling light into the valley and washing down the road, turning the yellow clay to gold. Instantly, the air grew warmer.

And then it occurred to him that what he'd felt were the eyes of his *abuelo* looking down on him. His *abuelo* had been dead longer than Eloy had been alive. Even so, Eloy had grown up feeling that he knew him. All his life everybody in his family had talked often about his beloved *abuelo*, Esequiel.

When he was little, these stories had finally brought his *abuelo* to life, until little Eloy could practically see him sitting across the kitchen table smiling, looking very much like the man in the faded black-and-white photo with the brown and yellow stains that his *abuelita* kept by her bed. After that, his *abuelo* had been Eloy's best friend and Eloy had talked to him whenever he was afraid or lonely. He even remembered a time when he'd been lost, when he felt his *abuelo*'s hand take his own and lead him home. It had been quite a shock when Eloy discovered other people couldn't see or hear or feel the *abuelo* who was so clearly visible, so real, to him.

Eloy smiled and turned around, the canteens banging heavily against his thighs. He hadn't felt his *abuelo*'s presence for a long time. It was a good sign, warming him more than the sunlight.

As the sun rose higher, Eloy knew he had to hurry before Pedernal woke up and some nosey neighbor asked him what he was doing—tipping over garbage cans, perhaps?—or dogs began to bark or chase after him. It must now be after six o'clock. Just before the road twisted left, Eloy scrambled up a steep bank to his right and half-pulled himself up the side of a large hill. Years ago, somebody had flattened the top of the hill for a house, but the house had never been built. From this spot Eloy could see everything around except what was directly below.

Eloy couldn't see Pedernal and Pedernal couldn't see him. But down where Pedernal was supposed to be, Eloy heard a dog begin to bark. And then another one.

He shuddered.

THREE

AS ELOY CAUGHT his breath and clapped dirt off his hands, he looked to the west, across the Río Grande valley. The sun was burning bare spots in the snow patches on the Jémez Mountains, spots that Eloy hadn't noticed a couple of days earlier.

Eloy looked down into the valley. From where he stood, the Río Grande itself was invisible, marked only by cottonwoods growing along its banks. The trees were shrouded in a faint green mist of new leaves. On the near side of the valley, windshields glinted between the rumpled foothills as cars went north and south on the busy four-lane highway to Española. Most pilgrims followed that highway until they turned off the smaller, winding road that went to Chimayó, but Eloy turned to look north. He'd been told that his *abuelo* had cut across the foothills, across Indian land, taking one of the trails that had been almost wide enough for two donkeys walking side-by-side as they carried loads of firewood from the mountains.

Eloy knew where the trail started that led north to Nambé Lake and then to the road to Chimayó—and he wanted to follow in his *abuelo*'s footsteps. But that trail was not used much these days. Eloy knew because last year he'd decided to run away from home with Felix, to live off trout and to steal from campers around Nambé Lake, and that's the way they tried to go. After walking for hours in zig-zagging *arroyos* and along trails that suddenly slid off hillsides, they'd started back. It took them until dark to find Pedernal.

Being lost like that had scared the beans right out of them. And they'd forgotten to take toilet paper.

Going toward the highway was shorter and seemed safer to Eloy. Even so, he hated being a chicken about taking his *abuelo's* route. Suddenly, he heard the loud, angry bark of a dog, seeming to come up the side of the hill on which he stood. It sounded just like one of Jesús Anaya's upholstery-eating pit bulls.

His legs made the decision for him and he found himself scrambling down the hill toward the highway, away from the approaching dog and away from a memory exploding in his mind.

But the memory was faster than any dog. As he slid down the hill, leaning back and cutting the air with his arms, he pictured the pup from a couple years ago that he'd seen some people dump from a car before gunning off down the road. The pup had sat, dazed, cringing by the road. The canteens pounded against his thighs, and he thought of the way he'd called the pup over. Eloy had fallen in love. He'd wanted a dog since he was three or four, but his *abuela* had always said no. "They don't do anything but make dirt and more puppies," she said whenever he asked. As he and the *perrita* played under the cottonwoods along the Río en Medio, Eloy had fallen more deeply in love and had tried to think of reasons why his *abuela* should let him keep her.

The hill suddenly fell away more steeply and he leaned back, almost sitting to slow himself. For a moment he thought of letting go his sack of food so the dog would eat that instead of him, but his hands were in such tight fists he couldn't. His breathing was now louder than the barks, but in his head he could hear the barks from two years ago as the Montoyas' dog charged out from the road to its house, teeth bared and eyes aimed at the pup Eloy had decided to adopt in spite of *abuelita*. As his feet plowed through the hillside, Eloy remembered the pup skidding to a stop and squatting in fright, puddling the dirt, just before the Montoyas' dog grabbed the pup in its mouth and crushed it.

"No!" Eloy cried, just as he'd cried that afternoon so long ago. "No!" And he felt the tightness in his chest that he'd felt when other dogs from Pedernal came flying down the road to join the Montoyas' dog, playing tug-of-war with the puppy's body. When the dogs were done, there had been nothing left of the pup. Nothing.

Now, two years later, both hatred and fear burned again in his throat as loosened rocks clattered down the hill ahead of him. Even though pebbles, sand, and dirt filled his sneakers, the moment he reached the bottom of the hill he began scrambling up the side of the next hill.

It was halfway up the hill that he noticed the silence. He half-sat, half-stood on the hillside, looking back, gulping air and trembling. Maybe the barks bouncing between the hills only made it sound like a dog was chasing him. His anger and hatred and fear gave way to relief. Jesús Anaya's pit bulls were not dogs you would want to be chased by, especially if you liked the way your face looked and the way your hands worked.

Eloy stood. Needing both hands for climbing, he jammed his bag of food down the neck of his shirt. It settled to where his shirt tucked into the canteen belt. As he moved, he tried to keep this new potbelly from bouncing.

The next several hilltops were strung together on sagging ridges that were half the width of his foot in the middle. Eloy found that the faster he walked the easier it was to keep his balance. When he reached the fifth hilltop he saw below a crowd of hills that shimmied as the shadows shrank and shifted in the growing light.

Leaning back, Eloy crab-walked down the hill. As he slid and slipped he knew that he wouldn't do this for anybody except for his *abuela*. He wouldn't be eating his own dust or snagging the bottoms of his jeans on little bushes or dragging his canteens on rocks for his father or brother. At one time he would have done anything for them too but not now. He kept his back slightly arched and peered over the mound of his stomach.

As the sack slid back and forth he felt a slickness that could only be mustard or mayonnaise oozing from the tortillas, leaking through the bag. He knew that he wouldn't put up with that for anybody but his *abuela*. Not even his mother. But then, his *abuela* had been his mother in many ways.

He loved his mother. It's just that she wasn't the one who took care of him when he was sick or hungry or bored. Eloy knew that his mother had to work, especially when his father was between jobs, and maybe more especially to get out of a house that wasn't hers, where her mother-in-law was the boss. His mother tried to spend time with him when she could. But there was a stiffness about her, a nervousness about being with him, that Eloy never felt with his *abuela*. And his mother didn't understand him the way his *abuela* did. Getting away with things with his mother was a game Eloy enjoyed. His mother waited until he did something wrong and then, if she caught him, she would punish him. But he didn't play games of wrong or right with his *abuela*. She often knew what bad things Eloy was going to do, even before he did them. Because she knew him so well, his *abuelita* often stopped him from getting into trouble, saving them both a lot of grief. She knew him that well—and yet she still loved him.

Eloy's mother did the best she could and most of the time he appreciated that. But her attention was like her cooking. When his *abuela* allowed her to cook, his mother's food didn't soothe the tongue or stomach the way his *abuela*'s did.

And she didn't make him feel as special as his *abuela* did. Eloy was terrified that his specialness would die with his *abuela*. He couldn't imagine life without her, without her love, her scolding, her joking, her care, and he was determined that she was not going to die—at least not yet—not if he could help it.

Anyway, his parents had been wrong to not let him make the pilgrimage for his *abuela*. Sure. He'd never before walked seventeen miles all at once. But they should have known he would do anything to keep his *abuela* alive. He'd walk barefoot over broken glass if he had to. Or eat dirt. Or beg God. Or risk a beating for disobeying his parents. After all, he *had* to do something. He would never be as important to anybody else as he was to his *abuela*. Nobody would ever care for him as much, or in the same ways, just as nobody would be able to make *natillas* that were so good his tongue seemed to soak up the flavor, leaving very little to swallow.

These thoughts carried him down the hill. Once at the bottom, he checked on the sack in his shirt and was relieved to see that what he'd felt was the paper sliding back and forth on his own sweat, not mustard.

The hills were smaller than the ones around Pedernal, but they were almost straight up and down, in waves slippery with sand and clay. He scrambled up, moving almost as if he were swimming, and then slid down. Each time Eloy reached the bottom of a hill, he felt that he'd moved backward in time. Even though the sun was slowly climbing higher, the dim, cool moments before dawn lingered between the hills. And each time he climbed out of these valleys, it was as if he climbed into another dawn. Dawn, dusk, dawn, dusk. Eloy soon felt as if he'd been scrambling up and down stupid little hills for days and nights and days.

On the top of each hill, he looked toward the highway for the glint of windshields. Each time he was disappointed that the highway looked just as far away as it had the last time. Maybe just a little closer, he tried to encourage himself—but not much. At last, he began to hear the faint roar of trucks and cars.

Eloy stopped in the cool of an *arroyo* at the bottom of a hill. His mouth was dry. Sitting in the sand, he unclipped a canteen and unscrewed the top. The top fell to the end of its chain tether, where it bounced against his throat as he drank. Water from these canteens always tasted like it had been squeezed from old socks. Eloy didn't mind so much because he imagined it tasting like the water Japanese guards had given his *abuelo.*

Clipping the canteen back into place, Eloy noticed that the sand between his feet was peppered with bright red rocks about the size of his thumb. He picked one up and spit on it. The color deepened. He'd seen rocks this color before, but never so many all by themselves in blonde sand. They made him think of drops of dinosaur blood, petrified where they might have fallen millions of years ago. Standing, he put three of them in his pocket.

And then he felt it again—the sensation of being watched. The sun was up. *Brujos* should be hiding and ghosts should be back in their *camposantos.* And Eloy had lost the feeling of being close to his *abuelo* many hills ago. A little way back Eloy had noticed several holes dug into *arroyo* walls. He wasn't afraid of coyotes the way he was afraid of dogs. But why would one be following him now? Eloy looked at his sack-filled shirt for the answer.

Picking up his pace, Eloy glanced over his shoulder, hoping that nothing was following him after all.

FOUR

THE DOG WASN'T a puppy but it wasn't grown up either. It was a medium-sized dog with short hair, mostly bluish gray among spots of black. The moment it saw Eloy stop and turn around, it dropped to the ground, resting its head on its paws. Eloy hesitated as he bent for a stone.

It was something about the dog's eyes. The dog appeared to look at Eloy with some fear, but seemed to be hopeful too. Its tail beat so gently that Eloy didn't know if it was wagging or if a breeze was ruffling its hair. But there was no breeze.

Eloy's heart thumped. He hated dogs ever since the Montoyas' dog had killed the puppy. His eyes narrowed in anger. "Scat!" The dog lifted its head and cocked it. The corners of its mouth lifting into a smile as it began to pant. Dog smiles angered Eloy.

"Get out of here!"

The dog closed its mouth, but only for a moment.

"Look, *pendejo*," Eloy continued. "I don't know if you're a bitch or a son-of-a-bitch." He quickly made the sign of the cross in penance for his profanity. "And I don't care beans, so *get . . . lost!*"

The smell of rolled up tortillas seeped into his thoughts and Eloy looked down. The sounds from the highway could almost have been coming from his pot-belly stomach. As he stared at the dog, his hunger and his hatred of dogs came together. "Eat your heart out," he said, wanting to sound as hard, as mean as his brother.

Eloy scrambled on top of a large rock that had been slammed up against the *arroyo* wall. The dog didn't move except to lower its chin onto its paws again. As he pulled the bag from his shirt, Eloy studied the dog. Was it a stray or did it belong to somebody? It didn't have a collar, but that didn't mean much. Lots of dogs around Pedernal didn't have collars. It wasn't too skinny. And another thing: it wasn't afraid of him the way a stray should be.

If it belonged to somebody, where did it come from? Not Pedernal. With exaggerated motions, Eloy pulled a rolled tortilla from the bag, pinching the far end of the tube to keep goop from squishing out, and lifted it toward his mouth.

"This is gonna be go-o-ood!" he taunted. The dog lifted its head, eyes locked onto the food, following the tortilla upward with such concentration that Eloy laughed. He moved the tortilla left and the dog's head swiveled. He moved it right and the dog's head swiveled again.

And then he remembered. In the past, always on Good Friday, his *abuelita* insisted that the family fast all day. It was a church law, but church laws were eas-ier to ignore than his *abuela.* "How can you eat, know-ing that Christ is dying for you with nails in His hands and nails in His feet and wearing a crown of thorns?"

she asked last year when she caught Eloy eating a Snickers. "How can you eat, *m'jito,* knowing that soldiers are piercing His side with a spear . . . probably at this very moment . . . and calling Him names?" The candy had turned to chalk in his stomach.

Even so, he'd gripped the candy and said, "But look, *abuelita,* Christ did all that two thousand years ago. Not today. He's not dying on no cross today."

His *abuela* had merely snatched the uneaten candy from his hand, glaring at him. She didn't say any more, knowing by the look on Eloy's face and the heat fanning through his ears that she didn't need to. She knew that he was feeling just the way she wanted him to feel.

Now, the smell of mustard had his saliva running and Eloy swallowed several times as he lowered the tortilla to his lap. The dog's eyes followed the tortilla's movements precisely—it was almost cross-eyed with staring so hard.

Eloy swore again and then cringed. Looking up at the sky he crossed himself and hoped that God understood. The word had felt good to say, sliding out the way it did. Plus he had a half-good reason for saying it. He wouldn't be able to eat now. He needed all the help he could get for his *abuela* and he felt as if his *abuela* and God had teamed up now, expecting him to fast.

He wished that he could swap the sin of swearing twice for the sin of eating. He wished he hadn't remembered about the fasting at all, or that he'd remembered after he'd eaten and there was nothing he could do except ask God's forgiveness or maybe stick a finger down his throat. It was too late now. And Eloy didn't think it would be wise today to commit this particular sin and ask forgiveness, all at the same time.

Eloy squinted at the dog. "If *I* can't eat this, *you're* not gonna eat it either," he announced.

Standing on the rock, Eloy reached above his head and scooped a hole into the clay and sand of the *arroyo* wall. Crumbs of clay and clotted sand fell down the collar of his shirt, gathering where the canteen belt encircled him. Stuffing the sack inside, he turned to face the dog.

The dog hadn't moved from where it lay, but its head was cocked upward, looking at the hole in which he'd put the food. Its ears were pressed back in alarm. A tiny whine rose from its throat and, startled by its own sound, the dog looked at Eloy, a mixture of shock and sadness showing in the way it held its ears.

Scrambling off the rock, Eloy looked once over his shoulder as he walked away. He saw the dog jump onto the rock in one smooth move and stand on its hind legs, reaching for the sack. Its paws fell at least six inches short.

As the dog danced on top of the rock, growing more frantic with each hop, Eloy saw it was a bitch.

It felt good to be on his way again, walking toward Chimayó. But the hills were still playing games with him. Despite the noises, the highway was farther than Eloy expected. He broke into a trot, holding down the canteens with both hands. The sand and dirt in his shirt ground against his skin. He kept on, buoyed by thinking each step was taking him closer to the Santuario, to the holy dirt that would cure his *abuela.*

He tried to concentrate on his *abuela* and his mission but couldn't get the dog off his mind. Where had it come from? Against all reasoning, Eloy couldn't shake the feeling that the dog had been following him all the way from Pedernal. After all, he'd felt something watching him when he first started out. Also, one of Jesús Anaya's dogs had been chasing *something* in anger, not just hunting a jack rabbit. Sometimes dogs got separated from their hiking masters in the Santa Fe National Forest and ended up in Pedernal. And there were those stupid people from Santa Fe who dropped off dogs in Pedernal not knowing what could happen to strays.

It occurred to Eloy that maybe this dog had been the one messing with the garbage cans. Maybe she'd been hiding in the hills, coming out at night to raid the garbage cans when the other dogs were sleepy with full bellies. She looked smart enough and fast enough to pull it off when other dogs couldn't. Maybe . . .

And then it happened. Eloy stepped from the shadows of the *arroyo.* Bright light blinded him for a moment and he stopped. Squinting, he saw the highway just a couple hundred feet away. And along the highway a thin but steady stream of people were walking north, trucks and cars roaring past them.

All *right!* he thought. He'd made it to the highway without getting lost! Until that moment, he didn't realize how much he'd been afraid of blowing this part of the pilgrimage, how much he was afraid he would prove that his parents were right after all.

And then, from behind, Eloy heard the soft panting of the dog.

FIVE

ELOY SPUN AROUND. "Go home!" he shouted. But instead of running away, the dog sat and looked at him patiently.

"Look, you . . . you . . . *dog!*" He bent over, this time determined to throw a rock. Most dogs ran before he could grab something. But when Eloy looked up the dog still sat, her chin lifted and to the side as if daring him to throw what he had in his hand, seeming to know he wouldn't.

Eloy's shoulders sagged as he straightened his back and let the rock drop next to his feet. "Stupid bitch," he muttered, and then wearily crossed himself. "Have it your way," he said, glaring. "And I hope you get run over by a car." Climbing out of the *arroyo*, he stepped over the sagging barbed wire of a fence, almost bumping his shins on a wooden cross, a couple feet high and painted white. It was a *descanso,* a marker pounded into the dirt by the relatives and friends of somebody who'd died on this spot, probably in a car wreck. There were several *descansos* on the windy road to Pedernal from Tesuque and Eloy had known two of the people whose names were on them. One of them had been Benito's best friend, before Benito had grown sour.

Eloy stepped around it. A name was carved in the wood, but he couldn't read more than a couple of letters because plastic flowers were draped over the crosspiece. It was spooky to stand where somebody had died. And it looked new. Eloy backed away, crossing himself, stepping toward the highway's shoulder where a line of pilgrims walked.

Some of the people he saw were old. Some of them were young. One woman carried a bundle in her arms, pressed against her chest. How long would she go before her baby grew too heavy and her arms felt like falling off?

As he watched, he suddenly felt shy about joining these people. He'd put on all clean clothes this morning, as if he were going to church with his *abuela*. And he knew one thing for sure—nobody had a better reason to walk than he did. After all, he wasn't walking for himself. He was walking for his *abuela*'s life.

In spite of feeling shy, he knew he must join them. All by himself he would never get God's attention. Eloy watched, impressed by the numbers of people walking by. God couldn't help noticing so many—and that meant Eloy should be part of the pilgrimage to get noticed. At least that's what he figured.

Even so, Eloy hesitated. If his parents had discovered he was gone this morning, they could catch him along the highway before they went to work. In fact, he wouldn't be surprised if his father was cruising up and down the highway right now, looking for him.

What time was it, anyway? Until eight or eight-thirty, Eloy wouldn't feel safe. He was willing to wait until he was sure his parents were at work. But maybe his parents didn't know he was gone. And the more he waited, the later he'd get home. If he got home too late his parents would find out for sure.

Should he wait? Or take a chance? He tried to wait, but when he couldn't stand it any longer, Eloy scrambled up the highway's shoulder and took his place in line.

The moment he began to walk on the asphalt skirting of the highway, his left shoe began to squeak. Not just a little squeak, but a loud one, as if he were killing a mouse with each step. For the moment, Eloy forgot about his parents.

He tried stepping all different kinds of ways to keep the shoe from squeaking—rolling forward on the outside, placing his foot down toes first, turning it in like a duck's and out like a chicken's. His shoe always squeaked, drowned out only by the sounds of passing vehicles. Finally, he stepped to the side. Sitting, he pulled his shoe up to his face to see if maybe a rock was jammed up into part of the tred, grinding against the pavement.

It was then he saw the dog had followed. It sat in the ditch alongside the highway, as if waiting for him to walk again. Eloy tried to ignore her as he studied the sole of his shoe. Seeing nothing, he untied his laces and tightened them closer to his toes, hoping that would work.

It didn't. As he walked, Eloy wondered why it was squeaking now, when it had been quiet coming down the hills from Pedernal. Maybe the squeak was God's punishment for saying and thinking and feeling some of the things he had this morning. Or maybe it was God's punishment for disobeying his parents, even though they were wrong. But that seemed ridiculous.

Why would God make his shoe squeak when He had better things to punish him with? What about the cars or pickups or semis passing him? Each semi dragged along ribbons of wind that snapped at his face, flicking painfully at his nose and eyes, setting his hair to fluttering. And some of the cars and pickups drove too close to the shoulder on which the pilgrims walked. It wouldn't take much—cigarette ashes dropped on a lap or a spilled Coke—for a driver to swerve and make road-kill out of him.

The squeaking was beginning to drive Eloy crazy. And on top of that, three times Eloy thought he heard his father's pickup coming from behind. I should have worn a hat, Eloy groused—one of my father's or one of my brother's. He hated to wear hats—he fought wearing them, even in winter—and his father or mother wouldn't have looked twice at a boy wearing one. By not doing something to disguise himself, Eloy was proving something his father was fond of saying, especially after he'd had a beer or two: "Life is just a bunch of mistakes. Even success is just a mistake making a mistake."

Eloy hunched over as he walked, bracing himself against the shock of the noise and the wind and the smell of exhaust of each passing vehicle. He tried to ignore the sound of his shoe. He tried not to listen for the sound of his father's pickup. And he tried to ignore the dog, who continued walking down in the ditch alongside him, looking like a distorted shadow on the wrong side of the sun.

Trying so hard to ignore these things, Eloy had forgotten about the other people he was walking with. Suddenly, right ahead, was a man with a huge walking stick. Eloy wondered if this man's reasons for walking were as good as his own. He couldn't help thinking that God couldn't answer *everybody's* prayers at one time—especially if they were each as difficult as his own. Father Ribera often said that God was all-powerful, but Eloy couldn't help feeling his prayer was in competition with the prayers of the other pilgrims.

Eloy picked up his pace. The man was humming and Eloy heard the wandering notes only when he was within a step or two of him. The sound was worn and deep, like the hum between songs coming from the frazzled speakers in his brother's low-riding car. It was then, too, that Eloy's nostrils tingled with the smell of the aftershave this man wore. It was a kind that smelled vaguely of booze. Maybe it was. He took a deep breath and put on a burst of speed.

"Hello there, *amigo.*" The man's voice rumbled.

Startled, Eloy looked up. The man was older than he looked from behind, with his smooth walk, narrow hips, and black hair, combed back and shiny, like fresh paint brushed on. "Hello," Eloy replied.

"Gonna be a hot one *¿qué no?*" The old man smiled at Eloy in an easy, generous way.

Eloy nodded and half-smiled back at this *viejo.* Suddenly the man frowned. "What's chasing you?" The man's eyes darted knowingly toward the dog.

"Nothing." Eloy looked at the dog too and saw that her ears were back, her teeth were bared, and her tongue was drawn into her mouth so it wouldn't get in the way of business.

"I heard a rumor that the finish line is in Chimayó somewhere. Is that true?"

Eloy didn't like the way this man was talking to him.

"Listen, *muchacho*. Forget this racing around. If you race with the Devil, the finish line is never where he says it'll be. Besides, the first one to the Devil's finish line . . . " And then he made a cutting motion with his finger across his throat. Chuckling, his eyes grew friendly again, as if he'd just told Eloy a very funny joke.

Thinking this *viejo* might be crazy or drunk or both, Eloy walked by, trying not to look as if he was hurrying, even though he was.

"That Devil, *muchacho,* he will fool you every time," the man said in a voice that sounded as if he was talking to himself instead of to Eloy. "*Con Díos.*" And then he began to hum again. After a few more steps, Eloy was thankful he could no longer hear the man, except for the *thunk, thunk* of his walking stick against the pavement.

It didn't take many steps to catch up with a woman who walked tipping back and forth on her feet, as if each step hurt. He didn't need a burst of speed to pull alongside her. He stole a sideways glance and saw the beads of sweat clinging to the fuzz of her upper lip. He wondered what she was walking for—legs that worked right, perhaps? Even for God that might be impossible. She continued to stare straight ahead and he left her behind gladly.

It felt wonderful to pass people, to work his way up in the line, where God would get to him before He ran out of energy or patience or both.

Up ahead and across four lanes of traffic Eloy saw Camel Rock. Camel Rock was a hill like any other hill, except that on one end it sprouted a squat sandstone neck on which balanced a long flat rock. It looked sort of like a camel—an old, sick camel anyway, unlike the one pictured on the packages of tax-free cigarettes his father liked to buy from the Tesuque Pueblo Indians at the Camel Rock Trading Post.

Eloy hurried by the trading post, once more afraid of being caught by his father and mother. Was this on the way to the landscaping job his father had now? He hurried, listening for his father's pickup, until he came upon a large group of pilgrims all in a bunch. They were laughing and talking loudly and for a moment Eloy didn't recognize that the words they used were Spanish. Although he didn't speak much Spanish, Eloy had grown up listening to his *abuela* speak it. He understood most everything she said when she talked with her old childhood friends in Pedernal, or when she muttered Spanish to herself as she worked. But now, overhearing these people, Eloy found there were many gaps in his understanding.

But of course, he thought. That was the way some Mexicans spoke—so fast they swallowed whole syllables and then belched them out while speaking the next.

They completely blocked Eloy's way. And they were talking too much and having too much of a good time to ever notice him. They might as well have been a large tree fallen across a river. And, unlike the water, Eloy couldn't go under them or over them. He could pass them on the left only if he stepped into traffic. And he could pass them on the right only if he dropped off the highway's shoulder and into the ditch, where the dog continued to shadow him.

The cut grass alongside the highway looked pretty flat and smooth, at least good enough for walking. Just one thing bothered him. He didn't want to give the dog the wrong idea by joining her. She might take it for a sign of friendship.

Eloy shook his head. Who cares? he thought. It's a free country. She can think whatever she wants, but that won't make it come true.

SIX

FROM THE HIGHWAY the ditch had looked smooth enough for easy walking. It wasn't. The grass was just long enough to hide holes, rocks, and garbage. He avoided some animal bones—maybe it had been hit by a car and then crawled off to the side to die. Or maybe they were just chicken bones, courtesy of Colonel Sanders. He barely avoided stepping on a disposable diaper, folded over and taped closed. And there were lots of bottles.

Eloy tried to concentrate, wanting to hurry past the group of Mexicans but not wanting to step on anything that was sharp or rotting. He tried to concentrate, but he couldn't help noticing the dog from the corner of his eye. The way she held her tail and head made her look pleased that he'd joined her.

With so many broken bottles in the ditch Eloy thought it was a miracle she hadn't shredded her feet. Eloy stepped around a flask. Next to it was a quart bottle of whiskey and one of gin, something Eloy had never tasted but had always wanted to try.

"¡Híjole!" Eloy muttered, picking his way through the garbage.

Looking up, Eloy saw that the Mexicans were a little farther ahead than before. "Shi—" He closed his mouth, biting the word in two.

God knew what he thought and God sat in judgment. Eloy glanced upward, hoping just this once that God was watching and listening to somebody else. He broke into a run, almost stepping on a carcass that looked like it had once been a cat, or maybe a skunk. A cloud of flies, swarming up from the carcass, went for his nostrils and eyes and ears.

He waved at the flies, clamping his mouth shut and holding his breath. He saw a ring of broken glass, teeth coming up from the bottom of a bottle like an unsprung trap, only after he'd put down his foot. A tooth caught the bottom edge of his jeans and he shook his leg as if the glass were trying to bite him.

"Hey!" he shouted, swatting at one last persistent fly. It was then he realized that he didn't hear talking above him. Eloy looked up and saw all the Mexicans directly above, silent, staring at him with great interest as they walked. One of the women looked concerned, as if Eloy might be having a fit.

With all those faces looking at him, Eloy blushed, feeling now as if a fit might be coming on. He stumbled on a plastic milk jug, almost falling. And then he began to run, without the cooperation of his legs, which seemed to have lost their bones. And a good thing too, because he might have broken a bone or two when he tripped and fell, landing on a Blake's Lotaburger bag stuffed with greasy garbage. Picking himself up, he tried to continue running—it felt more like swimming upright, away from a drain sucking at his feet.

It didn't help that the Mexicans cheered for him now, with a few claps thrown in.

"Pobrecito," said one of the men. Walking as fast as Eloy ran, he slid partway down the embankment reaching out an arm.

Eloy grabbed the hand, so calloused that it felt hard and cold and slippery, as if it was also holding marbles. Eloy grabbed and felt himself pulled upward, toward the cheering. Below him the dog barked and growled.

The man smiled and patted Eloy on the shoulder. He nodded toward the ditch. "Some *perra* you got," he said with a heavy accent. *"Muy bonita."* He chuckled, as if he'd just told Eloy a joke. The dog continued to bark, more frantic now, lunging closer to the man. Eloy saw the hackles raised on her shoulders and over her butt. Their eyes connected for a long moment, the dog's and Eloy's, and the dog reluctantly slowed her barking and finally stopped. But her hackles remained up, and her ears down.

"Thank you," Eloy mumbled, turning back to the man.

"De nada." The man was shy now, ushering him along the road's shoulder in front of the group.

Eloy walked as fast as he could, trying to remember what dignity felt like. The canteens smacked against his thighs, a half-step behind his feet and his shoe began squeaking again. He found it difficult to walk with any grace at all. These Mexicans were undoubtedly listening to his shoe and watching him, wondering what stupid but interesting thing he was going to do next—crawl on his hands and knees to Chimayó perhaps, kissing at the ground every few feet, like some pilgrims supposedly did?

His palms tingled from when he fell, and he looked at them. Dirt and little pebbles stuck to his skin.

Impatiently, he patted and brushed his hands against the thighs of his jeans. In a flash, the dog bounded up the highway's shoulder and was by his side. She gave the back of Eloy's hand a quick lick—a dry, feathery lick—and tucked in beside him.

Shocked, he stepped away from the dog, almost stepping into traffic. "Scat!" He chopped at the air by his canteens with his hands, looking back to make sure the dog kept its distance. She fell back, but kept pace with Eloy.

Why did things keep going wrong? Eloy listened to his shoe and the sound of a dog trotting behind him, wondering if things like this happened to every pilgrim or just to him. Had anything like these things happened to his grandfather? If his luck didn't get better, the next thing he knew his father would come by and see him.

What time was it, anyway? Eloy looked up at the sky. The sun was climbing higher and he tried to figure out what time of day it was. Surely it was after eight, but Eloy didn't know that for a fact. He walked faster, hoping time would go faster too. He was tired of worrying about his parents.

But for now he couldn't help worrying. He pictured it all—how his parents found out he was gone. He pictured their angry faces and the exaggerated way their mouths must have moved as they tried to speak softly, so as not to disturb his *abuela,* who heard anyway.

Why had they been so unreasonable? Why had they forced him to disobey them? Didn't they care about his *abuela?*

They cared. Thinking about it now, Eloy could see that something had changed with his mom and dad after his *abuela* got the cancer. Before, they'd argued some, but not nearly as much and not with such anger and bitterness. Before, his father hadn't been so rude and moody. And his mother hadn't been so bossy—as if she was practicing being in charge for when his *abuela* died. Didn't they know that helping his *abuelita* would also help them—help them return to being what they were before?

Suddenly, Eloy realized that he was not only walking for his *abuela*, but for his parents too—for their happiness. This new responsibility was like extra weight on his shoulders. Eloy felt increasingly tired but continued to walk as fast as he could. He didn't like that the dog kept up with him, along with the squeak in his shoe. He didn't like it but there was nothing he could do, which made him more tired still.

He continued passing people. Each time he passed somebody he felt a little better. And by the time he reached the Circle K in Cuyamungue, Eloy had passed thirty-three people and was feeling pretty good—good enough to ask a woman what time it was as he passed her.

She bent her neck downward instead of lifting her wrist up. "About nine," she said, wearily.

Nine! Eloy was relieved that it was after eight. But then it hit him. Nine? And he was only as far as Cuyamungue, from where he could practically see Pedernal!

Maybe his mother had been right. At this rate he'd never make it to Chimayó.

SEVEN

"¡HÍJOLE!" MORE DETERMINED than ever, he pushed against his weariness, toward the Santuario de Chimayó. So it was nine in the morning. So what.

What had Christ been doing at nine on that first Good Friday, anyway? Christ couldn't have been in too much of a hurry. Eloy pictured Christ dragging His cross through the streets of Jerusalem, no longer worried about getting splinters in His hands, because by now He had plenty of them—and big ones too. He was probably trying to keep His mind off the nails and everything else He knew was going to happen to Him at the top of the very last hill, which Eloy pictured looking like the top of a human skull.

What had Christ thought of His Father as He carried His own cross to the place where He was going to be killed? Eloy tried to picture what he'd been told in catechism. He knew that Christ had fallen a bunch of times—those were some of the Stations of the Cross—and that each time He fell He'd been helped. How many Stations of the Cross were there, anyway?

Eloy also remembered that Christ had been stripped. And Eloy knew that He had cried out for water and had been given vinegar to drink instead. But

Eloy couldn't remember if these were what made up the Stations of the Cross. He wished now that he'd paid better attention.

Cars and trucks zoomed by, kicking up dust that coated the inside of Eloy's nose. As the sun rose higher, Eloy began to feel uncomfortably hot. Strength seemed to leak out of him, drop by drop, sucked out with his sweat. He heard the dog's toe nails on the asphalt behind him.

Ahead, Eloy saw the line of pilgrims stretching toward Las Barrancas, which he could see even from Pedernal. These badlands of naked clay and sand rose from the valley floor and had always looked like the backbones of dinosaurs to Eloy. The line of pilgrims looked to him as if they weren't headed for the Santuario but to Las Barrancas instead, where their bones might mingle with the bleached bones of dinosaurs and of pilgrims from years past.

As soon as he thought this, Eloy regretted it. Surely this was not the kind of thing to think during a pilgrimage. Surely this was not the kind of thought that would impress God or make Him want to help Eloy's *abuela*.

But what was a pilgrim supposed to think about during a pilgrimage anyway? Nobody had ever told him and Eloy had no idea. He remembered the rosary beads but wasn't bored enough for Hail Marys and Our Fathers yet.

Instead, he figured he should think about his *abuela*. He wanted to picture her well again, after God took care of the cancer.

He pictured his *abuelita* from the top branches of an old apple tree in their front yard when he was six. He was screaming and crying because he'd climbed too high and was too scared to move. As he clung to a branch that swayed back and forth he saw her scurry from the house.

She looked up, her hands on her hips, studying him. "Okay, *m'jito*," she'd finally said. "How about you just hold on and I'll help you."

Incredibly, his *abuela* had tucked the bottom of her dress into the top of her apron. Eloy had never seen her bare legs before and they looked like a bird's, only uglier, being almost bone white with knotted blood vessels showing through. She grabbed the first branch and pulled herself off the ground with a monumental grunt. Wrestling herself up to the first branch, she panted as she decided her next move. When at last she was just a couple branches below him, she looked up, gasping as she smiled.

"Okay, now," she'd said, a wheeze still in her voice. "I'm gonna grab your foot and put it where it needs to go." She pulled his left foot down, almost yanking Eloy off balance, and set it on a branch that Eloy wouldn't have stepped on for a hundred dollars. He began to pull it up.

"Don't be a baby," his *abuela* scolded. "Step down." She tightened her grip and pulled on his foot.

Step-by-step, she'd guided him. When they both stood on the lowest branch she looked at him and said, "I can't make it to the ground without your help. If I jump now, I'm gonna break something. So get down there and do what I say."

As scared as he was, Eloy had jumped to the ground and then helped his *abuela*, taking care not to look up, under her dress.

Eloy smiled, remembering this. And then another, earlier, memory came. When he was five, he remembered sitting on his bed, hitting himself in the head. He'd been trying to discover how hard Felix needed to punch him before it hurt.

Eloy had started with little punches, not really wanting to hurt himself. But he forced himself to make each punch a little harder. Even when his right ear began to ring, he knew Felix could hit harder than that. He was about to hit himself again, harder, when Benito walked into the room.

Benito stared. "What the *mocos* are you doing?"

Eloy lowered his fist to his lap, grinning to hide his embarrassment. "I want to know how hard Felix needs to hit . . . to hurt me."

"Oh," Benito said. "You two have another fight?"

Eloy nodded. He and Felix were enemies almost as much as they were friends.

"Want me to help?"

Eloy smiled. Together, he and Benito would make *refritos* of Felix. "Sure," Eloy said.

Benito sat next to him on the bed. "Okay," he said, making a fist. "Does this hurt?" To Eloy's surprise, Benito brushed his knuckles over the side of his head.

"No." Eloy giggled nervously, realizing now what Benito had meant by help.

"This?" Benito hit him this time, but gently.

"No." Eloy scrunched his eyes, waiting for the next hit. And when it came, he blinked.

"Did that hurt?"

"No."

The next hit made Eloy wince, but he didn't say anything.

Each punch got harder, until Eloy had to shut his eyes to keep tears from coming. "You got a hard little bean-head," Benito said, grunting as he hit again.

With that hit, tiny stars exploded in Eloy's head. His eyes popped open and a scream flew from his mouth.

"Now we're getting somewhere," Benito had said.

Abuelita had rushed into the room just as Benito's fist was raised to strike Eloy again. She ran up to Benito, grabbing his raised arm, and slapped him on the face. Benito had cried out in surprise more than pain. "He asked me to do it!" Benito shouted. "He asked me to hit him!"

Still holding Benito's arm, their *abuela* leveled her eyes on Eloy. He struggled to keep tears from falling. "Is that true?"

Eloy nodded, even though it wasn't exactly true.

"You asked him to hit you?"

Eloy nodded again, but not as hard. After all, Benito had tricked him.

"I don't even want to know why." Their *abuela* had sighed in disgust, letting go of Benito's arm. Almost tenderly, she brushed Benito's reddened cheek and then cupped their heads, one in each hand. Gently, she knocked them together. "Sometimes I think maybe God made a mistake when He made boys."

Without warning, another memory came. Not too long before his *abuela* was told she had the cancer, he'd sneaked into her bedroom. He'd closed the door, even though she was visiting a neighbor and Eloy didn't expect her back for a long time. He sat on her bed, one of his brother's cigarettes in his mouth and his *abuela's* purse on his lap, opened. He'd just bought basketball shoes—the ones he now wore—and was broke. He needed a few dollars and maybe some loose change to play with in his pockets.

Just as he reached inside the purse, his *abuela* had walked in. At first she saw only the cigarette. She'd stepped up to him, giving him a look that might have put out the cigarette's fire except that, in his surprise and horror, he'd sucked in his breath. The cigarette blazed and he'd choked on smoke that filled his stomach as well as his lungs. And when he coughed the cigarette dropped into the purse. Quickly, Eloy dumped everything in the purse onto the bed, brushing the smoldering cigarette onto the floor. He stepped on it before he remembered that his feet were bare. Luckily, fear had numbed him.

Eloy had been terrified to look at his *abuela*. Instead he stared at the wads of paper money and the coins and all the other things that had come from the purse. On top of it all was the wooden St. Francis his *abuelo* had made while a prisoner-of-war.

He waited for his *abuela*'s anger to scald his ears. He waited and when the silence became more painful than any of the words he expected, Eloy looked up. Her face was drained of blood, but her eyes were blazing. She turned around and walked from the room.

For the first time in Eloy's life, his *abuela* didn't say anything to him for several days. For those days, he'd felt as if he held the entire night sky inside his own body, the stars burning tiny holes in his lungs and guts and head.

His *abuela*'s silence had been like the silence of God after the few times he'd prayed in earnest. How would he know if God had heard his prayers? Maybe God heard them but chose to ignore them. Eloy could only assume that God's silence had to do with all the bad and sinful things he'd done and thought. He could only assume that he was not worthy enough for God to listen to.

It had been the same with his *abuela*'s silence. And then, when she did talk to him again, it was to tell him that she had the cancer and would be going to the hospital.

The pain of this memory was like a rock hitting him in the stomach. Why would anybody—especially God—listen to him, after all the horrible things he'd done and thought and felt? Eloy couldn't blame God for ignoring him in the past. But now was different. He was walking for his *abuela*. God had to listen.

From what he'd learned in catechism and heard in church there was one, sure way to get God's attention. Eloy needed to suffer. For the first time in his life, Eloy wanted to suffer. God seemed partial to suffering.

What should he do? Pick up a rock and bang it against his head? How hard should he hit himself to get God's attention, to make God happy? Harder than Felix? Harder than Benito?

And then Eloy remembered the rosary. Saying the rosary was a way to suffer greatly. Besides, mumbling the prayers for the rosary was one way to get God's attention—in the same way a horsefly always got Eloy's attention, buzzing and buzzing. He reached into his pocket, groping. Instead of the rosary, he felt one of the little rocks he'd found in the *arroyo* earlier that morning.

Sweat from his body had darkened its color. *Blood of Christ,* Father Ribera's voice said in his head, startling and clear. Eloy stared, seeing a fossil of Christ's blood in his hand instead of a red rock. It was creepy. He almost expected the rock to melt into real blood as it lay in his palm, becoming a button of blood in the same place the nail went into Christ's hand, flowing down his life line and onto the ground, thick as melting candle wax.

It was a frightening thought, and probably sinful. Eloy threw the rock as far as he could. He didn't realize how slowly he was now walking until he saw that the last person he'd passed was up ahead. Maybe it was from not having breakfast. Maybe it was from being too careful with his water. Maybe it was from all the things he'd been thinking. Whatever the reason, Eloy didn't have the energy or desire to pick up his pace.

Another person passed him. And then he felt pressure, gentle but firm, against the outside of his right leg. Looking down, he saw the dog nudging him with her shoulder, herding him. The dog looked up and when their eyes connected she took his hand in her mouth.

EIGHT

WITH HIS HAND in the dog's mouth, Eloy sensed the power of her jaws. The dog's tongue pulsed as she breathed, pulling air around his fingers. He knew the dog could do some damage if she wanted. Clenching his teeth, trying not to imagine what she could do, Eloy let the dog lead him along.

After a few minutes he eased it from her mouth, cautiously twisting his hand back and forth. Once it was free he looked at her, appreciating her gentleness—she could have hurt him and she didn't.

Why had this dog chosen to be with him, of all people? He looked at the top of the dog's head, for the first time allowing himself to accept that this dog was going to follow him whether or not he wanted her to.

"Have it your way." He surprised himself by talking to her. Her ears pricked up.

He took a deep breath and began walking fast enough to move ahead of the two people who had just passed him. Passing yet another person, he settled into a nice, easy rhythm. Looking up at the cloudless sky, he noticed an airplane crossing the valley, sunlight glinting from its wings, dragging behind it a white trail. When he was little he used to wave at airplanes, imagining the people inside waving back. He'd stopped doing this when Benito told him that nobody in airplanes could see him, that they were too far up. Now, as he walked, Eloy wondered if God was too high up to see a person on the ground.

Suddenly, the dog began to growl, deep and loud. And a voice came from behind.

"Hey!" The voice was young and high. And scared. Eloy looked over his shoulder. The boy wore wild-colored pants, baggy and loose, a black T-shirt, and a pair of high-top basketball shoes. The boy looked as if he were about nine, but wishing he were sixteen. "Will your dog bite?"

The boy scowled at the dog. Eloy was about to tell this boy that she wasn't his dog. Instead, he surprised himself by saying, "No."

The boy nodded as his face broke into an uneasy smile. In spite of Eloy's answer he kept Eloy between himself and the dog as he stepped onto the asphalt skirting of the highway.

"How many people have *you* passed?" the boy asked.

Eloy studied the boy, wondering if he was mocking him.

"I've passed sixty-eight," the boy volunteered. "You're sixty-nine." He looked at Eloy, giving him the once-over, not looking especially impressed with what he saw. "Where did you start from?" he asked.

Eloy squinted at this *mosca* who thought he was a boy. What business was it of his? "Santa Fe," he lied. "Where did you start from?" Eloy wanted to take control of this inquisition.

"Camel Rock." And then the boy's eyes narrowed,

as if he'd been tricked into admitting something that wasn't good. "My father, he couldn't find his car keys this morning and we didn't leave Albuquerque until . . . oh, about eight."

Liar, Eloy wanted to say. Instead, Eloy picked up his pace, hoping to leave this boy behind. The boy matched him step for step.

"What's your name?" the kid asked.

"Eloy." And then he felt stupid. "Archuleta," he added, using Felix's last name.

"You can call me Ramón," the boy said, with a twist in his voice suggesting that it was not his real name.

For a couple minutes they walked in silence, Eloy wondering who "Ramón" really was. Maybe his name was Harvey Wallbanger and it embarrassed him. Eloy waited to say something, letting the silence grow awkward. Is this what it would be like to have a younger brother? he wondered. Sometimes he wished he had a younger brother to boss around, especially since he and Benito weren't getting along these days. But if this was what younger brothers were like maybe it was better that his parents were too tired or too old or too whatever to make another child.

"What's your dog's name?" Ramón finally asked, smiling as if nothing was wrong.

Again Eloy's first thought was to tell the boy that the dog wasn't his. Instead, he said, "Magdalena"—not knowing exactly why, except that he had an Aunt Magdalena.

"So it's a girl," the boy said, bending over to look at the dog's underside. The dog growled and her hackles rose.

"Hey, look, Magdalena: no hands. I just wanted a

peek." Ramón waved his hands and skipped a half-step in front of Eloy for protection. "Not that you got anything great to look at." He turned to Eloy. "She do that to all the guys?" He grinned.

Eloy struggled not to smile—he didn't want to encourage this kid to keep walking with him. In the silence, his shoe seemed to squeak louder than before.

"You pay extra for your shoe to sound like that?"

Eloy ignored him, but Ramón didn't seem able to notice rudeness.

"Maybe you got something stuck on the bottom . . . you know, tar or a rock or something," Ramón suggested. "Or maybe something busted inside. How much did they cost anyway?"

That question was too much to ignore. Eloy's head jerked toward Ramón and he stared in disbelief. Asking questions like that, it was a wonder Ramón's nose wasn't growing sideways. These were the shoes that Eloy had saved money for a couple of months to buy, the shoes that had wiped him out and caused him to try stealing from his *abuela*, shoes that were now driving him crazy with their squeaking. "Plenty." He glared at Ramón's nose, which looked like an easy enough target. Ramón was too busy watching Eloy's shoe to notice.

Eloy knew that if he didn't ditch this kid he was going to end up doing some serious damage to his face, which was a sure way to get God's attention, but not the kind of attention that would help his *abuela*.

"Mine cost one fifty." Ramón kicked up his feet to give Eloy a better look, causing Magdalena to growl. Eloy looked at Magdalena gratefully. Ramón jumped and danced ahead of Eloy. "What's her problem, man? She got fleas in her brain?"

Eloy kept his eyes forward and didn't say anything, hoping silence would repel Ramón like bug spray. It was something his brother did often, and it usually worked. But then Eloy could never remember being as pesky with Benito as this Ramón was with him. Maybe it would take more than silence.

They were approaching an abandoned gas station on the right. "Hey, look," Ramón said, skipping ahead of Eloy and turning around to face him. He hopped and danced backward, pointing to the bashed-up pumps. "A Station of the Cross. Get it?" Ramón looked disappointed when Eloy didn't laugh. "You know, the kind of station where Jesus could make a pit stop too. Maybe get a candy bar." And he laughed again, as if to encourage Eloy to laugh.

When Eloy didn't respond, Ramón shrugged and turned around, letting Eloy catch up to him. Eloy remembered wishing that he was suffering. Being with Ramón would make walking to Chimayó seem like one-hundred miles, not seventeen. Had God listened and sent Ramón to help Eloy suffer?

They were fast approaching what looked like a family—a man and woman with a boy and a girl.

"Look at *that*," Ramón said under his breath, whistling softly as he breathed in. "That chick . . . too bad she's with her ol' man and ol' lady. M-a-a-an! Look at *that*." He winked at Eloy. "I'd love to get her in the backseat of *my* car. I'd teach her . . . Ooo-eeey!"

Eloy couldn't help himself. He laughed. He hoped that when he'd joked like that with Benito he hadn't sounded as stupid as Ramón just did.

Still laughing, Eloy looked at Ramón. To Ramón's credit, he didn't seem to mind Eloy laughing at him. Instead, Ramón smirked as they walked up to the family.

"Excuse me and my friend here," Ramón said in a grand voice, forcing it down low. Four surprised faces turned to stare at Eloy and Ramón. One of the faces smiled.

Eloy wanted to die. Barbara was in the next grade, but he'd sure stared at her plenty in school. *"¡Qué guapa!"* he used to say to Felix whenever he saw her. He was scared that she might hear him someday, at the same time hoping she would.

"Hi," she said to Eloy, sounding nice and friendly.

"Hi," he mumbled.

Then Barbara looked at Ramón. Her smile wilted.

Eloy frowned. Finally, one of the girls who starred in his dreams notices him and he's with this punk kid Ramón, who makes eyes at her and acts like an idiot. There was only one thing for Eloy to do.

"See you around," Eloy said over his shoulder, hoping he sounded cool as he tried to strut by, Ramón and Magdalena at his heels.

Jerk-face! he thought. Jerk-face *pendejo!* He glared at Ramón sideways, not wanting to look at him directly. He might have been able to walk to Chimayó with Barbara if Ramón hadn't embarrassed him. Maybe he would have gotten a ride back toward Pedernal with whoever was supposed to pick up her family. She probably thought that Ramón was his brother, for Chrissake!

Ramón looked at Eloy, a big smile on his face. "She

don't know what she's missing . . . a handsome dude like me."

Eloy threw Ramón the evil eye. *Pendejo.*

They walked in silence, Eloy more determined than ever to ditch this kid. How? Before he could think of anything, Ramón broke the silence.

"Why you walking, man?"

The question surprised Eloy, but before he could tell Ramón it was none of his stinking business, another question popped from Ramón's mouth. "Know why I'm walking?"

Eloy stared at this kid who had so much guts that there wasn't room for all of it where his guts were supposed to be. His head must be filled with leftover guts instead of brains, Eloy thought.

"My father," Ramón answered himself, before Eloy could say anything. "My father, well . . . he's trying to stop drinking and he asked me to come and I thought it might be fun . . . meet some chicks . . . you know. But he's so *slow,* man. And this is so boring." He looked up, his smile melting when he saw Eloy's stony face. "I know," he said, his voice suddenly nasty. "Let's get a gun, man. We can put your shoe out of its misery. And your dog too."

Ramón skipped ahead of Eloy and Magdalena, making a gun out of the fingers of his right hand. He pointed at Magdalena. "Pow! Pow!" Magdalena growled. The barrel of Ramón's pretend gun recoiled each time he shot and his laugh was harsh as he turned, half-walking and half-trotting down the road.

It was hard, but Eloy held back. Any other time he would have made the little *pendejo* show some respect. But now Eloy watched as Ramón put more distance between them. Sometimes, Eloy thought, to ditch somebody you have to let them think they're ditching you.

When he was about twenty yards ahead, Ramón looked over his shoulder. He yelled something that Eloy didn't understand. But he did understand what Ramón was saying with his middle finger.

Magdalena growled, which is what Eloy wanted to do as he watched the wild colored pants get smaller and smaller, their colors mushing together. Eloy was relieved to be alone again.

The highway began to climb. Las Barrancas were now to his left. At the top of the hill the highway curved right, wrapping around a hill that rose above Pojoaque with its fast food joints and gas stations and the Butterfly Springs Mobile Home Park. The mobile homes looked like the cars of a derailed train except that between them laundry fluttered on lines.

He unhooked a canteen from its belt, unscrewing the lid and drinking as he walked. He had to admit he was getting tired. And the armpits of his shirt were uncomfortably stiff with dried sweat. Was he a third of the way through his pilgrimage? How much longer did he have to listen to his shoe and the traffic and to walk, walk, walk? How much longer was he going to have to think only good thoughts? Did God enjoy watching people suffer? Eloy knew that God made the rules, but the way it was beginning to seem, God made rules like a bully makes rules.

As Eloy screwed on the canteen's lid he hoped God hadn't been listening to his thoughts just now. Looking over his shoulder, he saw the dog was close to his feet, her tongue hanging out, looking dry.

Kneeling off to the side of the highway, he

unscrewed the lid again. Even as he cupped one hand and held it out to the dog, Eloy was amazed that he was doing this thing. But she had helped get rid of Ramón. And maybe this would impress God—make up for some of the things he'd thought today.

"Come here, Magdalena," he said, his voice flat, trying not to sound friendly or unfriendly. He poured a thin stream of water into his palm.

The dog stepped up to his hand and licked at the water, her tongue growing bolder as the stream grew fatter.

NINE

HIS STOMACH SLOSHED as he walked. Rounding the hill's flank, Eloy heard water running, gurgling like a toilet that needed its handle to be jiggled. He felt cool air coming off the Nambé River before he stepped onto the bridge.

Below, several ropes of water ran down the middle of a flat bed, hissing as they snarled and unsnarled. On the other side of the bridge, the four-lane highway continued north to Española and the smaller road to Chimayó branched off to the right, following the left bank of the river, aimed toward the mountains. Eloy hoped he'd walked six or seven miles so far, but he couldn't be sure. Those little hills at the beginning had probably slowed him down a lot.

Along the riverbed, large cottonwoods towered above an undergrowth of russian olives and tamarisk, box elders and elms, all of them just leafing out. Eloy didn't realize how beaten down by the sun he was until he stepped into the cool, high tunnel made by these trees. The road was criss-crossed with ribbons of shade tossed down by branches.

Pedernal wasn't far away, but winter was bolder in the mountains and spring was more cautious. Here, off the highway, next to the river, new grass hid the bases of trees. Ahead and across the road, Eloy saw daffodils and red tulips in a front yard. Draped over a coyote fence were fluttering patches of white flowers, delicate as the old lace scarves from Spain his *abuela* kept in her *trastero*.

As he walked, the roar of trucks and semis and cars grew faint, replaced by bird calls and the sounds of the river. Eloy guessed there were as many people walking along this road as there had been walking along the highway, but he felt more private here. Above him, the sky looked like pieces of broken blue glass held together by branches. It reminded him of the huge windows in the cathedral in Santa Fe.

Feeling more private, Eloy felt closer to God. Now that there weren't so many distractions, maybe he could pay better attention to God and maybe God could pay better attention to him. Was God looking now? Eloy glanced upward. Was God like one of those surveillance cameras in a convenience store? Perhaps. Like God, those cameras caused him to think guilty thoughts even when he wasn't shoplifting. Looking down from the brightness of the sky, the shadows of tree branches seemed to float just above the ground, ruffled by the breeze.

As Eloy looked around, he thought it strange that there weren't dogs out by the road, barking at all the people walking by. In Pedernal, the dogs would have barked until they lost their voices and then continued, forcing strangling sounds from their chests. Maybe the people who lived in the houses that looked over this road kept their dogs inside, knowing that pilgrims walked by on Good Friday. He glanced at

Magdalena, who seemed lost in peaceful thoughts of her own.

Cars passed him slowly and quietly. But on the narrow road they drove closer to the shoulder than did cars on the highway—so close Eloy could tell who smoked and who didn't by a smell like the one surrounding Benito's bed this morning.

Just beyond the first few houses, Eloy came upon many cars parked alongside the road, in the shade of the undergrowth. Eloy stared at these cars with some disgust. People who started this close to Chimayó were cheating. They weren't as serious or as worthy as pilgrims who walked from Santa Fe—or from Pedernal. He hoped God was taking notes.

Some cars were pulling up now, nosing into gaps too small for a car to fit without doors scraping paint. He passed a man and woman standing in front of the open trunk of a Cadillac. The woman had on shorts and a halter top that didn't cover the straps of her bra. As he walked by, Eloy caught a glimpse of her watch, oversized and white with big, black numbers—a watch for people who needed glasses but were embarrassed to wear them. It was only ten fifty.

He grinned, feeling as if he'd made some serious progress in the past hour. Maybe he'd make it to Chimayó after all.

It was then that Eloy sensed Magdalena was no longer at his side. He looked over his shoulder, hoping to see her lagging, perhaps baffled by the parked cars. He was surprised to feel his heart thumping as his eyes darted here and there, searching for her among the patches of light and shadow that camouflaged the road ahead. He wanted to call her name, but she couldn't possibly know it—he'd only said it to her once. Maybe, he thought, she's on the other side of the parked cars. He searched the spaces between parked cars, just as he used to look down the aisles in the grocery store when he was separated from his *abuela* or his mother. He was beginning to feel as if *he* was lost, and not the dog.

What if she'd found somebody who had food or who was friendlier with her than he had been? The thought made him feel jealous. Sure, he hadn't fed her—at least not from his hand—but he had given her water from his *abuelo's* canteen. A worse thought came to him: maybe somebody had stolen her.

And then, up ahead, he saw her run from between two parked cars, looking both up and down the road, water streaming off her coat. She saw Eloy and bounded toward him. And then she leapt, taking his forearm in her mouth, so gently that Eloy barely felt her teeth. Letting go, she landed on her feet and shook.

He held his arms over his eyes. "Hey, stop it, Magdalena. Stop it, you little *moco!*" He tried to sound angry but it felt too good—her coming back to him and her pleasure at seeing him and the water splattering, cooling him.

When she was finished she sat in front of him, her backbone wiggling, looking up.

"Come on," he said, patting his thigh as he took a step. It felt right for her tucked in beside him.

They walked, Eloy enjoying the shade and the sounds and the smells—and for the first time allowing himself to enjoy the dog's company. They walked through a haze of sweetness and Eloy saw a small apple tree in blossom down by the river. It was sure to get zapped by frost, having flowered so early, but Eloy breathed deeply, enjoying its mistake.

A low-rider drove by, a red Chevy Impala, its engine rumbling and, true to what it was called, its body dragging dangerously close to the road. The car's windows were tinted black. Sitting in a car with tinted windows was wonderful. His brother's car was like that. It was dark and private—you could see everybody outside the car and they couldn't see you. And why not? Even Benito had some modesty and didn't want everybody looking in to see what he and his girlfriends were doing or not doing when he parked or drove along.

Eloy admired the chrome and the beautiful paint job on the Impala as it pulled away from him. His brother would have loved seeing it and if his brother had been with him now, he and Eloy might have talked about low-riders—what they liked and didn't like, what they hoped someday to own.

Thinking this, Eloy remembered a game he and his brother used to play a couple years ago, when they were still buddies. They used to sit on a hill outside of Pedernal after school, looking down at the road going to the village of Río en Medio, making comments about the cars going by.

One spring Benito's teacher read *Tom Sawyer* to her class. Every afternoon as they watched cars, Benito told Eloy what had happened in the part she'd read that day. Eloy loved it.

One afternoon his brother said, "You know, that man Mark Twain . . . the guy who wrote *Tom Sawyer* . . . he came from a place where they ate people." Eloy had looked at his brother sideways, not reacting, not knowing if his brother was joking. "Yeah," Benito continued, serious. "He came from a place called Cannibal . . . I forget the state."

Just then a low-rider had come cruising by, dragging its tail, its purple paint so dark that the tinted windows almost blended with the rest of it.

"*That's* the kind of car Mark Twain would drive . . . if they had cars back then," Benito had said reverently, almost whispering. "He'd go driving by and if he saw somebody who looked good and juicy, he'd stop and ask them to jump in and how could they say no? And then he'd take them back to Cannibal and eat them."

After that, when they saw a car, they'd try to match it with somebody famous they'd heard about in school. Jesus Christ drove a VW Bug without fenders. Abraham Lincoln hated Lincoln Continentals. Instead, he drove a green Jeep with a car phone. Christopher Columbus drove a red Ford truck with a double cab. And Benjamin Franklin drove a school bus, its muffler dragging, sending out showers of sparks so he could study electricity.

Eloy smiled as he thought of that. It had been nice when he and his brother were friends. His smile turned to a frown. What had gone wrong? Was it his brother's friend dying on the road to Pedernal? Was it something he, Eloy, had done? Whatever the reason, Benito didn't spend time with Eloy anymore and Eloy wouldn't want him to, anyway. Benito was too much of a hot-shot—too cool, too mean, too stuck-up even to let Eloy help him work on his low-rider. "I know dogs who use screwdrivers better than you," Benito said once to Eloy. Their father, overhearing this, had laughed before scolding Benito. That laughter had made Eloy feel that perhaps his parents felt the same way as Benito. Did God laugh at Eloy too? Was his *abuela* the only one who thought Eloy was special?

He saw Magdalena out of the corner of his eye. She thought he was special. It warmed Eloy to see her tuck in closer to him when they approached people to pass, brushing up against his legs. Sometimes the people said hello. When they made nice comments about Magdalena, Eloy smiled back and nodded his head, agreeing, taking credit as if she belonged to him.

Eloy kept passing people, working his way up in the line of pilgrims. He was feeling good about his progress. He wasn't even bothered by the squeak in his shoe all that much anymore. But each minute was beginning to seem like the last. Looking ahead, he was beginning to think he'd seen each stretch of road before.

He was bored. Bored, bored, bored—bored enough for Hail Marys and Our Fathers. He reached into his pocket, past the rocks of fossilized blood, and pulled out the rosary.

It was a simple rosary, made of wooden beads. On the front of the wooden cross was glued a silver figure with its arms up and out, so small there were no details on the face. It could have been anybody's face—Eloy had once even imagined it was his own—but, of course, it was Jesus Christ.

Eloy made the sign of the cross, cupped the beads in his left hand, and took the cross in his right hand. As he raced through the Apostle's Creed he remembered the times his *abuela* made him sit in the kitchen while she cooked so that she could listen to him practice his prayers.

"Hail Mary," she'd begin, and Eloy would launch

into the words, racing his *abuela* to finish "now-and-at-the-hour-of-our-death-Amen." He didn't have a chance to win when she wanted to say the prayers in Spanish. But in English he beat her most every time. She'd look at him with a challenge in her eyes and say, "Our Father . . . " That was Eloy's cue. He raced through the kingdoms come and the daily breads and the trespasses—all in one breath—sometimes barely making it to "but-deliver-us-from-evil-Amen" before he ran out of air.

Unlike Father Ribera, his *abuela* didn't care if Eloy understood what he was saying. She just wanted him to know all the words in their correct order. And fast—the faster he could say prayers, the more she liked it. Eloy pictured his *abuela* in her bed the other night, fingers moving over the beads, lips moving but not with any particular word. It was as if she breathed out a used, worn-out Hail Mary and then breathed in a fresh one, full of hope.

When he finished the Apostle's Creed, Eloy looked at his hands. He couldn't remember what came next. He fingered the first bead above the cross, puzzled and upset. Should he say a Glory to the Father? He messed up a couple of words, but when he got to the end of that prayer he rattled off an Our Father. Next came three beads attached close together, in a bunch. That meant he was supposed to say the same thing for each of them but he didn't know what it should be. Taking a stab, Eloy said three Hail Marys.

He wished now that he knew what to do, that he didn't have to look at the stupid beads to tell which ones were attached close together and were for the same prayer and which ones were farther apart and meant something different. Eloy was angry at himself—and at God for making things so complicated. He decided that God could just take it or leave it. Clutching the beads, he hoped that God knew he was doing his best.

It was then he heard a familiar rumbling approach from behind. Benito's car sounded like that. An odor Eloy recognized advanced with the sound—a combination of oil and burning rubber and hot metal too.

TEN

ELOY STUFFED THE rosary into his jean pocket. If he was hearing and smelling his brother's car, he didn't want his brother to see him with the beads.

He looked down at Magdalena and saw that her hackles were half-raised. "It's okay," he said, his voice unsure. Her hackles remained up.

Whoever was driving the car suddenly popped the clutch and gunned the engine before shifting down. It was something his brother often did. He reached toward Magdalena but she was quicker than he was, licking his hand before he could touch her.

The car didn't pass, continuing to shadow him instead. Why was this car polishing his shoes with its fender? As he listened, Eloy decided this car needed tuning and a ring job—just like Benito's.

Why would his brother be doing this to him? Was he checking up on him, making sure he was all right? Didn't he think Eloy could make it? Didn't he think he was strong enough or determined enough?

The car continued to follow and Eloy heard Magdalena growl. If his brother was checking on him, he was taking his sweet time. It was as if Benito wanted to get on Eloy's nerves. Or maybe his brother was giving Eloy every opportunity to give up, break down, and beg for a ride back home.

"We'll make it," he told Magdalena. "I'm gonna get that holy dirt and I don't need that . . . that armpit's help."

Eloy remembered his brother's mocking smile the other night. Most likely Benito had heard the entire argument he'd had with his parents and, while his brother had been out partying last night, he'd hatched this plan with his friends to bother Eloy during the pilgrimage.

This morning, Eloy thought, I should have stepped closer to Benito's car when I took a leak. I should have aimed for a window in case it was partly open. I should have written my name on the driver's door.

And then another thought struck him. Didn't Benito know that he, Eloy, was walking for him too? Didn't his brother realize that life would get better at home for everybody with their *abuela* well again and back to her old self? Didn't he know that their father wouldn't be so nasty to everybody, including Benito, and that his mother wouldn't be so bossy? Didn't he know?

The car's engine roared again and suddenly Eloy knew just what he should do. But before he could turn around and throw a rock at the windshield, the car pulled up beside him. It was his brother's car, all right. Eloy knew his brother was driving—his brother never let anybody else drive his car—even though it had pulled up too quickly for Eloy to see him through the windshield, which was the only somewhat clear glass in the whole car.

Even through the dust and grime on the windows, Eloy saw his own face reflected back to him. Maybe it was the dirt blurring his reflection, or the curve of the glass, but what Eloy saw was a face pulled this way and that with anger and fear. It made Eloy think of a dog with a shaved face.

Eloy suddenly hated the tinted windows he'd always admired, windows that made it impossible to see inside and that forced him to look at himself. He imagined his brother smirking at Eloy's anger, using the same mocking smile Eloy had seen the other night, tapping his fingers on the chain steering wheel to the music and . . .

But there wasn't any music coming from inside the car. *Nada.* Not even a little soft music for a girlfriend who straddled the floor's hump to be extra close. His brother usually drove with the music so loud it pushed the thoughts right out of Eloy's head. Eloy had always suspected the music also covered up the sounds of the sick engine. And when the bass was real loud, which was most of the time, Eloy suspected it helped jump start the car when it stalled at intersections, which was often.

Without music his brother would be able to hear every choice word Eloy wanted to shout. Throwing his brother the finger and shaking it so that it swiped at the glass of the front passenger's window, Eloy took a breath deep enough for everything he wanted to say. Just then, Benito popped the clutch, gunned the engine, and threw it into gear. Off he roared, like the chicken he was, in a cloud of smoke that was part burning tires and part oil burning instead of gas.

Magdalena tucked in a little closer, brushing up against his right leg every few steps. He looked down, grateful that she was still there. Next to her he saw his own hand, trembling. "It's okay," he grunted more than said, making a fist to calm his fingers. "Every little thing is . . . okay."

He didn't believe it, but what else could he say? Magdalena seemed to be counting on him.

As he walked his anger began to fade, leaving behind an aching emptiness not unlike a hangover. He shouldn't have thrown Benito the finger. It wasn't the right thing for a pilgrim to do on Good Friday. Benito had probably deserved it—but maybe he hadn't. Maybe Benito had the music off so he could talk to Eloy. The passenger door window was terrible to get down even for the passenger, and maybe Eloy hadn't given his brother the time he'd needed to get it down to tell him what he'd wanted to say.

Or maybe his brother had come all this way to offer him a ride back home after the pilgrimage—to help get him back before his parents got home. He'd thought of asking his brother for a ride but he'd been afraid of being turned down. And even if his brother said yes, he'd have made him beg.

Feeling this way diminished the beauty of this stretch of road. Was the beauty a trap, a way God tricked pilgrims into forgetting why they were walking? If God couldn't fix everybody's problems, maybe that was one way to weed out some of them.

For the first time, Eloy felt truly tired. He'd been walking uphill steadily since turning off onto this road. It had been gradual and everything around him had been so wonderful that he hadn't paid very much attention to it. Now the hill seemed to be fighting him a little with each step. Maybe his anger had taken some of the fight out of him. And he was thirsty, and with the thirst came a gnawing in his stomach. For whatever reason, a weakness was beginning to work its way into the muscles of his legs. The half-empty canteens felt heavier than when they were full.

He looked at Magdalena. "Aren't you tired?" he asked. She looked at him, her head held high. As he returned her gaze, Eloy was amazed to realize that not once since she'd joined him had he seen her sniffing at garbage or greasy spots along the road. It was as if she were walking not for pleasure but for a purpose. Was she on a pilgrimage too? What could she be walking for?

Up ahead, Eloy saw the end of the tunnel of trees. There the road climbed steeply and to the left, out of the river valley. Reaching into his pocket, he fumbled for the rosary and pulled it out. Slowly, working by feel, he tried to unlock the tangle of beads. Even his fingers felt puffy and tired.

The road grew steeper as it neared the curve. Eloy plodded along, bent forward, feeling a tightness in the small of his back.

The more he struggled with the beads, the more knotted they seemed to grow and the more knotted his thoughts became. "Come on, you lousy beads," he muttered. He felt a vague soreness in his legs, deep in the muscles, somewhere near his bones, as if his bones were heating up and slowly cooking the flesh around them.

As the rosary loosened, the road emerged from the tunnel made by the cottonwood trees. Sunlight peppered him with bullets of heat. Instead of blood, sweat popped out where the heat struck, especially on his face and shoulders. The sun was high now, blazing, scorching the colors from everything it touched. The hills looked flat, as if painted on paper. As the road climbed up and to the left, Eloy found himself entering a plateau of badlands. Stunted, thin-looking piñon and juniper trees grew here and there. A stubble of chamisa and sage clung to the dirt. Was this something his *abuelo* had seen when he walked?

The moment the rosary untangled, Eloy felt the tenseness in his own body melt. He looked down, deciding to start from the beginning, to do the best he could. If he couldn't remember this time what to say for each bead, he could just alternate Hail Marys and Our Fathers.

At least he knew the right way to start. Eloy made the sign of the cross.

"I believe in God . . . " he began. He didn't hurry the words. He wasn't racing his *abuela*. He had plenty of time. And with the sun beating down on the nakedness of the land, the words took on a meaning he'd never heard in them before. " . . . descended into hell . . . ascended into heaven . . . judge the living . . . the forgiveness of sins . . . life everlasting. Amen."

Eloy glanced downward and saw Magdalena looking at him, listening.

"Thanks, Magdalena." He cleared his throat, feeling awkward about talking to the dog. "Thanks for sticking around."

ELEVEN

EACH HILL SEEMED steeper and longer than the one before. Saying the rosary made time wobbly and distances dizzy. He stumbled up three long hills and through two rosaries, not getting the prayers right and unable to remember the Mysteries of the Rosary. When he was in doubt, he did Hail Marys. He figured he couldn't go wrong with them, but each Hail Mary blurred into the next and they were drying his tongue and the back of his throat. He let the beads dangle from his hand, giving them a rest.

Eloy grew so hot that he took off his shirt, draping it in the crotch between his right canteen and its belt. He felt cooler for a few moments but the heat returned, making his skin prickly, soaking downward, into his muscles. He remembered his father's words about getting sunburned, but ignored them. The sun was directly overhead. Eloy hoped it was more or less noon.

He began to see things around him that he would never have seen in his right mind—as if he were walking through a bad dream. The badlands were the color of brittle, yellowed newspapers, scrunched up and blown in piles against the mountains. Bushes began to look like blurry letters, forming lines that disappeared in folds and tears only to reappear farther up or down the hill, the words not making sense. As much heat came from the road as from the sky. As heat seeped through the soles of his shoes he felt the button of a blister under the ball of his left foot, working its way under his skin, making its own buttonhole.

On several of these hills were large crosses, built by *penitentes*, devout men who walked from hill to hill as if they were Christ Himself doing the Stations of the Cross. Eloy heard that *penitentes* sometimes beat themselves bloody and senseless as they went. Some of the crosses were as large as abandoned telephone poles without wires.

Even Magdalena appeared tired now. Her tongue hung long. But her ears rose when he spoke. "It's a hot one *¿que no?*" His voice was so dry and husky it reminded him of the *viejo* with the walking stick. Meeting that man seemed like a dream now. The two of them stopped for a moment as Eloy drank from a canteen, gulping so fast the water hurt going down. When he finished, he poured water into his palm for her. When he stopped pouring she licked at his empty palm, begging with her eyes.

"No," he said, swishing around what little was left.

A woman approached and Eloy clipped the canteen onto its belt as he began walking. It had been a long time since he'd passed anybody, but he hadn't been passed for a long time, either.

He remembered worrying that he wasn't suffering enough. That had seemed so long ago—at Camel Rock—and along the Nambé River. He'd worried about not suffering enough and now he was suffering. Eloy hoped God was satisfied.

What if my abuela *dies after all?*

The question came from nowhere, lifting the hair on the back of his neck.

She will not die. Not yet. He was feeling so spacey he didn't know if he said these things in his head or aloud.

As he trudged up yet another hill, past a *descanso,* he struggled to control his thinking, to keep stupid thoughts from coming to life. But by now, his thoughts had minds of their own.

What if his *abuela* did die? His father was right about one thing: nobody lives forever.

Lately, more often than not, he'd seen her sleeping on her back, her hands at her sides—as if she were laid out in a coffin. Sometimes when she slept, parts of her face jerked, as if in pain. Folds of skin would shrink, pulling other skin toward them. These spasms didn't last long, but when they happened Eloy saw many faces appear in his *abuela's* face, some of them frightening, some of them funny, most of them looking like somebody else.

Sometimes her sleeping face was relaxed, looking satisfied. It was this peaceful face Eloy wanted to remember always. It was this face he wanted her to wear along with the old black dress hanging in her *trastero,* holding in her hands the photograph of her husband and the rosaries she treasured because the Pope had blessed them.

Eloy closed his eyes for a moment and concentrated. "Hey, God," he said. "Save my *abuela* and . . . and I'll become a priest."

He opened his eyes, listening with his whole body for a signal that God had heard this promise. He'd thought once or twice about how much fun Father Ribera must have listening to confessions. Eloy thought he would enjoy hearing about all the sinful things people did.

But Eloy knew that his chances of becoming a priest were as good as his *abuela* letting Magdalena live in her house. He regretted making this promise as soon as it popped out of his mouth. He closed his eyes.

"You better let my *abuela* live," he muttered. His voice rose with each word. "If she dies I'll end up being a jerk like Benito . . . maybe even a *pachuco*." He opened his eyes cautiously, half-expecting God to strike him down for this threat.

But nothing happened. As he walked through the badlands, Eloy decided God wasn't listening. Maybe that was just as well. Eloy seemed unable to keep sinful, angry thoughts out of his mind. He seemed unable to control what he remembered. Maybe the sun was cooking his brain, turning it into lumps like scrambled eggs.

Eloy didn't want to remember—not on his way to the Santuario de Chimayó to save his *abuela* from the cancer—but it came to him anyway: the wake of his mother's father, Grandpa Amador Gutierrez.

At wakes people usually told stories about the person who was dead. Most of the stories were funny, some sad, and some of them were pointless because people tried to talk when they were drunk. But Grandpa Amador had not been a nice man and at his wake, very few stories were told. After the few funny and sad stories, all that was left were stories about how mean or insulting Grandpa Amador had been. Of course, nobody wanted to tell those stories at his wake—except his widow, Grandmama Dolores, who never showed affection toward her husband when he was alive and none now that he was dead. As she told stories, everyone grew uncomfortable—tense and silent.

Luckily, Eloy's mother and sisters had hired a *mariachi* band for the wake. When they began to play, nobody seemed to care that they were perhaps the worst *mariachi* band in the world. Everybody except Grandmama Dolores got up to dance, working hard to ignore the sour notes.

After a while, Eloy had gone into the bathroom, not to do any business, but to get away from the music. Feeling dizzy, he pulled the lid onto the toilet and sat, propping his head on his arms, thankful that the bathroom door muffled the sounds of the trumpet player.

Eloy thought he'd locked the door. So when his Aunt Sophía barged in, he almost slipped off the toilet lid in surprise. Her face was already flushed, so he couldn't tell if she was embarrassed to walk in on him.

"Oh," she giggled. Eloy saw her lean one way and then the other. Her breath seemed strong enough to peel paint off the woodwork. "Please, *señor*, don't get up." She giggled again. Walking to the tub, she hitched her skirt and stepped inside. She turned to him and winked. "Tinkle, tinkle!" She giggled again and pulled the shower curtain closed. Eloy would always remember its pink, yellow, and blue tropical flowers.

What he heard next could have been water shooting from the faucet, directly into the drain, but he wasn't sure. Embarrassed for his aunt he stood just as that sound stopped. The words "Flushy, flushy!" came next, followed by more giggles. A scream interrupted the sound of water spraying. His aunt threw back the curtain and Eloy was shocked to see her swatting at water from the shower nozzle, aimed at her head. "Turn it off! Turn it off!" she screamed. Terrified, Eloy had fled the bathroom.

"*Abuelita's* wake won't be nothing like that," Eloy told Magdalena, who pricked up her ears. And then he realized what he said. "But she's not gonna die, not now, so there won't be a wake anyway." Magdalena's tail drooped at Eloy's angry words. He felt like hitting himself. "*¡Pendejo!*" he muttered. Why couldn't he control his thoughts, on this day of all days?

Squinting at the road ahead, he saw more cars than before. Maybe people were sightseeing, curious to see pilgrims suffering through the hottest part of the day. Or maybe people were on their way to pick up pilgrims who'd already finished.

What time could it be if some people were finished? He looked at the sky. The sun was a large, wavering patch of hot. Eloy couldn't tell what time it was, but guessed it had to be at least one in the afternoon.

The rosary swung against his thigh with each step. Each whack meant that he was getting closer to the Santuario and the holy dirt and a cure for his *abuela*. His spirits lifted for a few steps. But what if the dirt didn't work? His spirits crashed to the ground. And even if the dirt worked, he'd have to say good-bye to Magdalena when he got there. If his *abuela* got well, she'd never let him keep her.

He reached down and Magdalena nuzzled his hand. Was there a way he could keep Magdalena, just in case his *abuela* died? Angrily, he pulled his hand away. "My *abuela* won't die," he growled. "She won't." Alarmed, Magdalena stepped away from him.

Eloy was furious with himself and his thoughts. God was probably flipping through brain after brain, just as Eloy flipped through TV stations to find a good program, flipping through brains in search of good people to help among all the pilgrims. What if God flipped to his brain during a thought about his *abuela* dying? Would he flip to the next pilgrim, just as Eloy flipped through mouthwash commercials?

Then he stepped on a wad of chewing gum. He tried to scuff it onto the road but instead managed to spread it around so that it covered even more of his sole. Had God put the gum there on purpose?

Do you feel closer to God, now that you're miserable?

Eloy had no idea where the question came from or even who asked it. But the words resounded clearly in his mind. Was God speaking to him? Eloy shook his head. No. As much as he wanted to be chummy with God, suffering made Eloy feel farther from God, not closer. And angry too.

"You better cure my *abuela*," Eloy threatened. And then his threat turned to pleading. "I'll leave the stupid dog. I won't try to keep her. Just help *abuelita!*"

He avoided looking at Magdalena. It would hurt to leave her behind. But maybe that was the price God planned to charge for His help. Maybe He'd given him Magdalena just so He could take her away. It seemed like something God would do.

Despair tightened his gut. Eloy pictured *abuelo* Esequiel as his *abuela* described him, trying to talk about his own pilgrimage: his quivering lips, his shaking fingers, his watering eyes. His *abuela* was convinced that he'd seen a saint . . . maybe even *el Cristo Negro.*

Eloy's lips were quivering. His fingers shook and his eyes watered. As he forced himself up the next hill, it occurred to him that perhaps his *abuelo* hadn't been overcome by feeling closer to God during the pilgrimage, but by the disappointment of feeling farther from Him. Maybe his *abuelo* hadn't seen *el Cristo Negro.* Maybe he'd prayed that he would and instead he'd seen nothing.

Nothing, nothing, nothing.

Maybe he'd felt just as Eloy felt now—angry and cheated. Maybe he'd been so ashamed of those feelings that he could never admit them, especially to a wife who imagined her husband touching the hem of a saint's garment.

Maybe the only person who'd been brought closer to God by his *abuelo*'s pilgrimage had been his *abuela.* And then, only in her imagination.

Eloy wanted to cry out in anger to this bully who was God. But he didn't get a chance.

TWELVE

THE MAN WAS partly hidden by the shade of a juniper tree growing alongside the road. *"Hola,"* he said. Eloy jumped and Magdalena began to growl.

Eloy's feet stuttered before he stopped. The man was an old, stooped *Indio*, his skin the color of the hills, his hair as black as crow feathers and pulled back into a pony tail.

"Hello," Eloy said, reaching down to reassure Magdalena.

"A hot one *¿qué no?"*

Eloy saw a weariness in this man's eyes. "Yes," he said, nodding. "It is."

"I wonder," the man said, shifting his weight from one foot to another, "do you have any *agua* in those canteens of yours . . . that you could spare?"

Eloy hesitated.

"That's okay," the man said, his face stiffening as he shrugged. *"No hay problema.* I'll ask somebody else."

Eloy surprised himself by reaching for a canteen. "No. Here," he said.

Careful not to touch his lips to the canteen, the old man tipped his head back and poured a stream of water into his mouth. Eloy watched as the man's throat seemed to catch a measure of water and then let it go.

"How much farther . . . to Chimayó?" Eloy asked, swallowing saliva as the man handed the canteen to him.

"Oh, I'd say about two, three miles . . . another hour or so. Not far." He smiled at Eloy and wiped his mouth with the back of his hand.

Eloy wanted to ask the time, but he saw that this *viejo* wore only an old, silver bracelet with a large turquoise stone. He clipped the now empty canteen onto its belt, amazed that he'd given this man water, pleased with himself and at the same time irritated. If the man was right, he wouldn't need the water. But if the man was wrong. . . .

"You're a good boy," the man continued. "God be with you . . . with both of you." He glanced toward Magdalena.

Eloy nodded. A numbness filled his body as he continued walking. He felt as if he was floating more than walking.

The distance of a mile didn't mean anything to Eloy anymore—measuring time and distance seemed impossible now. Eloy noticed several more *descansos* along the road. Did they mark places where pilgrims from years past had dropped dead? Eloy was too tired to smile at his own little joke. And he was too tired to say any more prayers. Eloy put the rosary in his pocket. In doing so, he felt the two remaining rocks he'd picked up before he reached the highway.

They clacked against each other as he rolled them around in the palm of his hand. He listened for a few minutes and then dropped them along the road, one after the other, as if they were drops of Christ's blood, falling as He made His way through the last Stations of the Cross.

Eloy looked ahead. A line of cars crept up the next hill. Was Chimayó on the other side of the hill, beyond this traffic jam? Had the old *Indio* been right?

He reached for Magdalena and she met his hand with her nose. He tried not to think about having to leave her.

The line of cars seemed to play tricks with him. Although cars were constantly joining it, the line didn't seem to grow. Eloy felt as if he were walking in place, walking and walking but not covering any ground. He walked like this for what seemed like an hour, occassionally drawing closer to the line of cars only to have it move away from him. Gradually, in the heat and the glare of the afternoon, the sound of idling engines grew louder.

"We're gonna make it," he told Magdalena, his voice a husky whisper. She looked up and wagged her tail a few times before returning her attention to the road ahead.

It took a long time to pass the first car. But as he passed it, Eloy remembered the way he felt passing his first pilgrim that morning. Now, it was wonderful to be going faster than cars.

Some cars had windows rolled up, which meant air conditioners kept tempers cool inside. Most cars had windows down. From those cars elbows hung out, almost brushing against pilgrims. Cigarette smoke drifted through the air. Eloy avoided staring at the people in these cars even though they were probably staring at him. A couple of the low-riders were too beautiful not to stare at. One was maroon, its many layers of paint so perfectly smooth that the sun seemed to penetrate inches of smokey color. The windows were down and a man in the passenger side tipped his head toward Eloy, his mirrored sunglasses flashing. The man's mouth formed the faintest of smiles.

A few cars beyond, Eloy came upon a car with giant, fuzzy dice hanging from the rearview mirror, one a little lower than the other, reminding him of bull testicles. He shook his head angrily. That wasn't the kind of thought he should be having, so close to the Santuario.

When he finally crested the hill, Eloy saw a village down below. It lay between the deep folds of two ridges, in a valley that was wide yet secret, open yet protected. Looking down on the cottonwoods following the valley's river, looking down on the houses and mobile homes and cars with their flashing windows, looking down on the greening fields reaching into the crevices of every hill, Eloy was reminded of a drained catchment lake on his uncle's farm. When the dam cracked, the water left behind branches and mud and cans and algae and bottles and fish, their scales shining like the car windows below.

Chimayó! It had to be.

He found himself running down the hill, just as other pilgrims around him were doing. A few of them shouted for joy. Just as he was about to shout himself, pain shot through his thighs and cramps grabbed his calves. He slowed himself, but the hill was steep, forcing him to walk painfully fast. His shoe was now making a sound like his whole body felt.

His canteens flopped lightly against his legs, reminding him they were empty. Pain jabbed him with every step as the blister on the ball of his left foot spread, feeling hot as melted tar. He looked back every few steps to make sure Magdalena was following.

Eloy didn't know exactly how to get to the Santuario, but he figured the pilgrims ahead would show the way. Finally, at the bottom of the hill, Eloy found himself walking along a road that wove through some houses and led to a small, dusty plaza, crowded with people. Children ran around, some of them carrying sodas and corn-dogs and burritos. Grown-ups were gathered in clusters, the men and women standing or sitting underneath cottonwoods or perched on low, adobe walls in front of houses. Nobody seemed to be going anywhere in particular anymore.

Eloy felt as if he'd just walked to the wrong place. The people Eloy saw didn't seem to have the right attitude for pilgrims. Many of them were eating instead of fasting. Several priests walked around through the milling crowds, scowling as if they didn't approve of what was going on either. But then priests usually scowled unless they had a reason not to.

It was with great relief that Eloy spotted two bell towers on the other side of the plaza. The Santuario? He walked toward the towers.

Up ahead he saw a line of people that went over a bridge crossing an *acequia*, leading to the building with the bell towers. Sure enough, it was the Santuario. He hadn't expected a line to get into the church but he took his place at its end. As he looked at the people around him, he wondered how many of them had done the pilgrimage, had earned the right to be in this line. Many of them didn't look as if they'd walked very far.

In a matter of moments, waiting in line became

more painful than walking. Moving only to shuffle forward every so often, his muscles began to harden. His legs ached. Surprisingly his arms were tired too. And his back. And his neck. Even his head.

To loosen his muscles, Eloy stooped and stroked Magdalena from the top of her head all the way down her back. He felt Magdalena's entire body shiver with pleasure. It was the first time he'd touched so much of her and, realizing what he was doing, he pulled away. Why was he torturing himself? He'd walked for the holy dirt, not for a dog. He had to get the dirt and hitchhike home and Eloy knew that people almost never picked up hitchhikers with dogs. And even if he got her home, he'd never be able to keep her.

Before he could close the gap that had grown in front of him, two ladies in spring dresses filled it for him. Each of them was wearing an Easter-like hat and high heels and each was carrying a rosary.

Eloy trembled with anger, expecting other people in line to be outraged. When nobody said anything, Eloy pressed uncomfortably close, crowding them, daring them to say something. When they held their ground, he prepared to bump into the lady closest to him. He wanted to send her into the *acequia*, to water the flowers on her dress.

But then Eloy saw Father Ribera walking toward him.

THIRTEEN

FATHER RIBERA'S SMILE was undeniably happy, but in a grim sort of way. As usual, his eyes seemed to see what you were actually thinking. Whenever Eloy pictured God in his mind, His face looked remarkably like Father Ribera's, only with a white beard.

Eloy stooped to pet Magdalena again, hiding his face, hoping that Father Ribera was walking toward somebody else. If the *padre* saw him, it would be only a short time before his parents found out what he'd done today.

"Eloy!"

There was no escape. Reluctantly, Eloy looked up.

"My son, how happy I am to see you here!" Father Ribera extended his hand.

Eloy stood and took the hand of the *padre*. Father Ribera was famous for shaking one person's hand while talking to somebody else. Sometimes you could get your hand shaken by Father Ribera for five minutes, unable to get away, all the while listening to his conversation with the person next to you. Some people claimed he did it on purpose, to make feuding neighbors talk to each other, through him. Others claimed he didn't realize what he was doing.

"I've been looking all over for you!" Father Ribera continued pumping Eloy's hand. How did Father Ribera know he was going to be here? Had his brother told? No. Not even his brother would do that. Or would he? Puzzled, Eloy studied the priest's face for clues. All he saw was a broad smile, showing yellowed teeth that the *padre* had left in God's care instead of brushing. "And here you are. Finally. A pilgrim! *¡Un peregrino!* A prayer . . . walking on two legs!"

Eloy nodded, wishing the *padre* would let go of his hand. "I made it. Me and Magdalena, here." And he nodded toward the dog.

Father Ribera looked down at the dog as if seeing her for the first time. Letting go of Eloy's hand he knelt. The cross around his neck swung wildly but, to Eloy's surprise, Magdalena's ears remained up as Father Ribera patted her head.

"All those times I've come into your house to visit your *abuelita*, I didn't know you had a dog," Father Ribera said, standing. "She must be a quiet dog . . . a good dog. But come. I have somebody for you to see. Somebody very important. *Muy importante, hijo de Díos.*"

Eloy allowed Father Ribera to usher him over the bridge of the *acequia*, toward the Santuario. He shot the evil eye toward the women who'd butted in line. They were too busy with their beads to notice.

Who was this important person? A policeman? His father?

Who cares? Eloy thought. Whoever it is, I'll get the holy dirt for *abuelita*. They can't stop me now.

But Eloy did care. He didn't want his walk to end in a fight with his father or a ride back home in the cage of a police car.

He followed Father Ribera, wondering and worried, staring at the frayed back of the black jacket the *padre* always wore. Father Ribera was a small man, not much taller than Eloy himself. Even so, there was an impatient, rough energy about him. He walked like a boxer—a good one.

At the large front door, Father Ribera said, *"Pardóname,"* and the people in line moved over. Eloy stopped and Father Ribera turned to see what the matter was.

"Can Magdalena come in too?" Eloy asked. He knew he had to leave her behind sooner or later. But he didn't want to now.

Father Ribera smiled and said, "The dog? Certainly."

Stepping into the Santuario de Chimayó was like stepping into that moment the sun disappears beneath the horizon, leaving in the sky its richest colors. The air was cool, even though it smelled of bodies and candles burning. The light was golden, coming from tall, narrow windows set high and deep in the adobe walls. Behind the altar was a carved screen, gilded, with *nichos* for saints and tall paintings. It seemed to glow separately from window light or candlelight.

Father Ribera walked down the aisle, not pausing to dip into the holy water and genuflect. Before following, Eloy dropped quickly to one knee, busy with his hand at the same time. Instantly, Magdalena was by his side, her head cocked as if in concern. Eloy patted her head as he stood. The squeak of his shoe seemed to echo and Eloy limped down the aisle, keeping his weight off that foot. He was so busy looking around he almost bumped into Father Ribera, who was now staring at the altar.

Eloy was surprised to see people shuffling past a

large pine box sitting on the altar. It might have been a coffin, except that it was piled high with dirt. People filed by, filling little plastic bags with its dirt. Holy dirt? Eloy had always heard that the holy dirt came from a miraculous hole in the floor of the church that never emptied regardless of how much people took from it.

He looked to Father Ribera for an explanation. The *padre* smiled. "I'll tell you a secret," he said, leaning toward Eloy so that his voice was barely a whisper. "The dirt itself isn't holy." Eloy's mouth dropped. He'd walked all this way for dirt that wasn't holy? Father Ribera put a hand on the top of his head, as if comforting him. "You're surprised? The dirt itself doesn't do the miracles. It is the people's faith in the dirt that cures . . . what they believe the dirt will do, *that* makes miracles happen." Father Ribera smiled and he winked at Eloy, his yellow teeth showing. "Come . . . over here," he said, motioning to his right.

Perhaps it was just his eyes getting used to this dark corner of the church. Or perhaps it was the shock of who he saw. But when Eloy saw Benito and his *abuelita* sitting at the far end of the front pew, he gasped.

"*¡M'jito!*" his *abuela* moaned, trying to stand. Benito turned to help, but Father Ribera interrupted.

"Benito, you and I have some work to do. We must find some more bless̩d dirt for the pilgrims. Come."

Benito looked up from his *abuela* and nodded. "Sure," he said. As he stood, Eloy saw the shadow of a smile on his brother's face. "You wave real good, bro," Benito said. "Nice . . . nice and friendly."

Horrified, Eloy now knew why there hadn't been any music coming from his brother's car. Horrified,

Eloy now knew that he'd yelled and thrown the finger at . . . at his *abuela!*

He blushed deeply and Benito struggled not to smile. Cautiously, Eloy looked from Benito to his *abuela*. She patted the spot where Benito had been sitting. *"Siétate,"* she said. When he sat, the canteens bumped against the wood, pulling the belt upward so that it dug into his skin. His *abuela* reached out a hand and placed it on his shoulder. It was then that Eloy realized he was in the Santuario without his shirt on. Her hands were cold, his bare skin badly sunburned. He flinched.

"Abuelita . . . I'm . . . I'm sorry I threw the finger at you but . . . "

She shook her head. "Hush," she said, and her fingers trembled. "Let us sit and enjoy being here . . . in this holy place . . . together . . . for a moment." She looked into his eyes until he could stand it no longer. He turned his head toward the altar and the people who were filling little plastic sacks with dirt. As he watched, Father Ribera and Benito came in from a side door, each carrying a bucket. They dumped dirt into the box, spreading it with the rims of their buckets before they left.

He closed his eyes, overwelmed by thoughts. He'd walked for his *abuela*, come all this way to get holy dirt for her because he thought she was unable to come herself, because she'd given up and didn't want to come. Yet here she was. He didn't know which he felt most: cheated or happy that she was here—here where he came to get holy dirt that Father Ribera said wasn't holy, dirt that the *padre* brought in by the bucketful. Dirt just like any other dirt.

When his *abuela* spoke, he expected scolding words for throwing her the finger. Instead, her voice was gentle.

"You have made me happy today, Eloy . . . happier than I've been since before your *abuelo* Esequiel passed away. He would have been proud . . . proud to know you followed in his footsteps. Maybe," she said, squeezing his shoulder, making him flinch again, "maybe some day you will know such . . . such *felicidad.*"

Eloy opened his eyes and stared into hers. He had questions and doubts and things to say . . . but no words.

"I know why you walked here. And you and I will finish the walk . . . together. But first I want to tell you something that you do not want to hear, *m'jito.* I want you to hear it and I want you to believe it, if not now then some day when you remember the words I say.

"I will die soon . . . maybe tonight, maybe next week, maybe next month. But I will die and I am ready to die. *Jesús Cristo* died on this day and it will soon be time for me. Very soon. And, *m'jito,* I will be so happy not to feel this pain. I don't want to leave you, Eloy. But you have made me happy today and when I die I will die happy, knowing that I have a grandson who will grow up to be a good man. A good man. Maybe even a man of faith."

The words, soft as they were, stung. "No!" he said, shocked at how his voice filled the Santuario. "You will not . . ."

She put a finger to his lips. "Hush," she said. "Hush. I will die. And when I die I hope that you will be happy for me. Someday. And I want you to know how much it means that you walked for me today. Look. Father Ribera told me something . . . and it's true. You didn't know it, not while you were walking, but you were also walking for yourself. Maybe even more than you were walking for me, you walked for yourself." Her lips trembled. "I will miss you, Eloy. And you will miss me. But what you did today makes it easier for me to go . . . to die." She stared at his stricken face. And then, looking very tired, she leaned forward, resting her head on his shoulder. Growing up, Eloy had rested his head on her shoulder many times. But never, not once, had she rested her head on his shoulder. And he'd never seen her cry.

Easier to go? Eloy had walked all this way so that his *abeulita* would not die, and instead he'd made it *easier* for her to die?

All the feelings of the day filled Eloy at once. He buried his face in his *abuela*'s hair and together they cried.

Eloy felt a hand on his bare shoulder. Looking up he saw Father Ribera's solemn face. Beside him stood Benito.

"It is time to finish your pilgrimage," the *padre* said.

Benito looked at Eloy. "We better get going, to beat Mom and Dad." A smile flickered at the corners of Benito's mouth. "You done good, bro. Real good."

Benito's words felt wonderful, but it was then Eloy realized Magdalena was not by his side. Panic must have shown on his face as he searched the floor and underneath the pew.

"She's over here," Father Ribera said, nodding toward the altar. Magdalena was stretched out in front of the altar, her front paws crossed and twitching with dreams. Pilgrims stepped over her to collect dirt.

With the help of Father Ribera and Benito, Eloy's *abuela* got to her feet. "Take this, Eloy. It is yours now." She placed something in his hand. "It is too heavy for me to carry any more, but you are young."

It was his *abuelo's* St. Francis, the one he'd made as a prisoner-of-war. Eloy's eyes filled again with tears. People made way for them to step in line. Just ahead were the ladies who'd butted in front of him, staring at him now in wonder.

Eloy's *abuela* did not bother with plastic bags. Instead, she pinched dirt with her fingers and, making the sign of the cross, put it in her mouth. She did this three times. Eloy followed her example swallowing the sand mixed with the dirt. The smell of earth rose through the back of his nose. Spring, he thought. Eating dirt makes a smell like spring.

As he turned to leave, Eloy knelt by Magdalena. He didn't want to wake her. He wanted to leave her as she slept. Eloy didn't think he could cry any more. But he felt tears coming again. Why was God doing this to him? Why, especially now that he knew his *abuela* was going to die anyway? Eloy felt that leaving Magdalena was unfair of God. How many hundreds of times had his father said that life wasn't fair? Now Eloy knew his father was right. He stood to go.

But Magdalena must have sensed his presence. Her eyes jerked open and she scrambled to her feet, looking confused. When she saw Eloy, her tail began wagging.

Eloy turned to Father Ribera. "Could you find some-body to take her, *padre?*" he asked. "She followed me . . . all the way, I think . . . from near Pedernal. She's a good dog. Her name . . . her name is Magdalena."

"She comes home with us."

Eloy turned to look at his *abuela.* He wouldn't have been more surprised if she'd sworn. Instead, she nodded. A smile crept over her face.

"Come on," Benito said, sounding nervous. "We gotta go. It's getting late and the traffic is bad and you want to beat Mom and Dad home, don't you?"

Magdalena kept so close that she almost tripped Eloy as they walked from the Santuario, into the bright light of the afternoon.

FOURTEEN

AS BENITO PULLED his car into his usual place by the low rock wall, Eloy was relieved to see that his parents weren't home yet. He didn't want to get into trouble, especially since he hadn't accomplished what he'd set out to do.

Magdalena had sat on the floor in front of him, her head in his lap, shaking still from what seemed like her first ride in a car. He patted her now, letting her know he knew how she felt, letting her know it was all right now. Until this moment, he'd felt as nervous as she was. "You're gonna have to stay out here for a while," he said, leaning toward her, "until we figure something to tell Mom and Dad."

His *abuela* was stretched out in the back seat and he turned to look at her. Benito had turned off the ignition but the engine still rumbled and sputtered, not wanting to quit. "We're home," he said and she nodded, her eyes still closed.

After he and Benito helped their *abuelita* out of the car and into her bedroom, Eloy hobbled on sore feet to the kitchen. He'd never been so thirsty before in his life. He drank six glasses of water, one right after the other. Unlike last night, he craved more even though it was almost more than his stomach could hold. It was as if his body was a dried sponge, still able to soak up water.

As he sat on a kitchen chair, Benito walked into the kitchen. "She's tired but she's gonna be okay," he said. Standing where Eloy had seen him last night, Benito stared at Eloy for a long second. "She's tough, our *abuelita*." He stared at Eloy some more. "Maybe next year we could walk together, you and me," he finally said.

"Yeah." Eloy fought against smiling. "Hey, thanks for what you did this morning, to keep them from noticing I was gone." As they'd driven back to Pedernal, Benito had told him about the argument he'd purposely started with their father to keep their parents from noticing. Eloy wanted to say more than thanks. He wanted to tell Benito how great it was to feel as if they could be friends again. But he didn't want to push it, to say too much, to embarrass Benito and cause his brother to pull away from him again.

"Sure." His brother took a cigarette from his shirt pocket. "I'll take some water out to your dog. Maybe have a smoke before they come home."

Eloy was stiff and leaning over took unusual effort. His feet hurt and the bottom of the blistered foot almost felt like it had scabbed onto its sock. He wanted to get the shoes off, release the pain contained in them. Instead, as each shoe came off the pain of each foot exploded, growing as large as the room before it began to shrink, to fade.

Eloy peeled off his socks and was relieved to see the blister hadn't broken. His relief vanished when he heard the sound he'd dreaded so much that morning—

the sound of his father's pickup. Silence followed, interrupted when his mother rushed into the house.

"Hi, Eloy," she said with hardly a sideways glance at him. "I can't wait to get out these clothes and into something clean . . . something that doesn't smell like that Mrs. Danskin's house."

As she disappeared into the hallway his father burst into the kitchen with Benito. Scowling, his father threw himself into a chair and leaned back so that it reared up on its hind legs.

"I've been thinking about it all day . . . about what you told me this morning . . . and the more I think about it the madder I get," his father said, staring at Benito, who leaned against his own shadow on the kitchen wall. "Now you know why your uncle sold you that car so cheap." White teeth flashed as Benito grinned toward Eloy. The chair's front legs slammed onto the floor. "I'm not stupid, you little *pendejo!* Now your uncle is going to charge us an arm and a leg to help pull the engine. All that work is going to keep him in beer for months. And all because you didn't listen when I told you that car was a piece of junk!"

Eloy couldn't help grinning back at his brother. It was true that Benito had probably been suckered into buying his car from their Uncle Julian. And it was also true that their uncle didn't help fix anybody's car for free—some people said he charged his own wife to fix her car. But he was the best mechanic around, so why shouldn't he? And Benito's car had potential.

"Look, Papa." Benito sounded bored. "Uncle Julian doesn't need to help. Why don't *you* show us how to pull the engine and what to do?"

Eloy almost laughed out loud. Benito was fighting

dirty, all right. His father was good with rocks and adobes and plants and cement, but he didn't know beans about cars. On the other hand, Uncle Julian had made his first car when he was twelve, out of parts from the junkyard.

Just then his mother walked into the kitchen. "Are you two still arguing about that car and saying bad things about my brother?" She stood behind Eloy and put her hands on his shoulders. His sunburn was feeling worse, not better. If I was a prayer walking on two legs, Eloy thought, I'm a sunburned prayer. And tomorrow I'll be a blistered prayer. "It gets boring, you know. Always about the stupid car and always about my brother."

Their father shifted his glare from Benito to their mother. "Where's dinner?" he asked.

"It's Good Friday and we're all fasting," she said.

"*Híjole*," their father sighed. "I break my back all day and when I come home there's no food on the table and no beer either."

Eloy felt his mother's fingers tighten on his shoulders and he shrugged to warn her not to squeeze too hard. Her fingers relaxed.

"Look. I just came in here to tell you to be quiet. We don't want to wake up your mother."

Just as she said this, Eloy heard shuffling feet coming toward the kitchen. He turned to see his *abuela* standing in the doorway, staring at him. Shrugging off his mother's hands, he stood and offered *abuelita* the chair. Slowly, walking as if her feet were as blistered as his, keeping her eyes on him, Eloy's *abuelita* sat.

"I hope we didn't wake you," Eloy's mother said. His *abuela* shook her head, her gaze never shifting from Eloy.

Eloy found it impossible to look away from her. Her eyes didn't move from his face. She sat motionless, not moving except when she blinked or when her eyes narrowed and widened. And still she stared.

"Are you feeling all right, Momma?" There was concern in his father's voice, a tenderness Eloy hadn't heard in a while.

It was as if she were deaf. She sat as if waiting, patiently waiting for Eloy to do something. But what? Slowly, it became clear what she wanted him to do.

But first he looked at his brother. His brother had gone to a lot of trouble to keep Eloy's pilgrimage a secret. Eloy didn't want his brother to be hurt or disappointed, didn't want to ruin his chance to be buddies again with him. One side of Benito's mouth went up into a half-smile and he nodded, giving permission.

With one last look to his *abuela*, Eloy faced his father.

"Papa . . . " He looked at his mother. "Momma, I . . . I walked to the Santuario de Chimayó today. I . . . I disobeyed you. But I walked and I made it. And Benito brought *abuelita* to meet me there. And Father Ribera was there and . . . "

His lips quivered and his fingers shook. Tears came to his eyes. How could he describe what he'd been through? How could he describe something that he didn't know if he understood himself? He'd walked. He'd made it. He'd eaten dirt alongside his *abuela*. But he knew now that she was going to die anyway—die in spite of his walk—that she was even going to die happier because of his walk.

What had he done? Anything?

What had he gained? Nothing?

Had God heard anything? Had God seen anything? Did God even care?

Blinking back his tears, he looked once more at his *abuela*. Her eyes were closed as she sat, but her face was lifted toward the ceiling and there was a smile on her face.

When he looked at his mother, he saw that there were tears in her eyes as well. "I made it, Momma." His voice was thick with feelings. She stepped toward him and reached out to hug him. This time Eloy didn't brush her off. "I made it," he said into her hair. "And Benito brought us back. Me and *abuelita* and . . . and Magdalena." He fought against crying.

The silence stretched to breaking. And then Eloy's father cleared his throat. His father opened his mouth to say something, but when nothing came out he closed it, his face showing confusion. Eloy had seen that look only once before, when his father accidently slammed a car door on some of Eloy's fingers. He wanted to say something, something nice, but his mother spoke before he could say anything.

"Your Aunt Magdalena?" She loosened her arms from around him and he stepped away from her. He saw on her cheeks the trails left by tears.

"No. A real dog." Everybody turned in surprise to Benito. "Cute, too." Benito smiled toward Eloy.

Eloy looked to his *abuela*. Her eyes were open now and she nodded encouragement. Sounding like his father, he cleared his throat. "Magdalena is a dog who followed me . . . walked with me all the way. We brought her back and . . . and I want to keep her."

And then his *abuela* spoke, a ferocity in her eyes but a softness in her voice. "Go bring in this *perrita* of

103

yours . . . this gift from God." She looked at Eloy's father. "Sometimes we ask God for one thing and He gives us some other things we might need instead. And sometimes He takes things away. He knows what He's doing."

Outside, in the fading light of the day, Eloy saw Benito's car. Surrounding the car were a half dozen dogs from Pedernal, some of them pacing back and forth, some of them growling, some barking, some of them marking the tires.

As he got closer, Eloy saw Magdalena inside the car trying to ignore the other dogs. She sat in the front seat behind the steering wheel, looking through the windshield as if she was driving. Eloy followed her gaze. She looked toward the garbage can with its lid sitting cockeyed on top.

Eloy picked up a rock. He missed the Ortiz dog but hit the left back door of Benito's car—which was just as well: the sound of the rock hitting metal was like a gun going off and the dogs scattered, becoming the shadows of shadows.

He walked to the car. "Come on, Magdalena." He opened the door and she hopped out.

Together, Eloy and Magdalena walked around the stone wall and the daffodils hiding diamonds, down the flagstone path to the back door of the house. They walked slowly and Eloy felt the liquid in his blister squishing around with each step. At least it doesn't squeak, he thought. The fingers of his right hand fiddled with St. Francis, who was tangled in the rosary. He wished now he hadn't thrown away the red rocks.

Maybe they had been dinosaur blood. Or Christ's.

He reached down with his other hand, his fingers searching. And then, soft as the brush of a feather, Magdalena's tongue slipped across his palm.

SPANISH WORDS AND PHRASES

abuela [ah-boo-ay'-la] grandmother

abuelita [ah-boo-ay-lee'-ta] little grandmother (affectionate)

abuelo [ah-boo-ay'-lo] grandfather

acequia [ah-say'-ke-ah] an irrigation ditch

agua [ah'-goo-ah] water

amigo [ah-mee'-go] friend

angelito [ahn-hel-lee'-to] little angel

arroyo [ar-ro'-yo] stream bed, dry except during rain

brujo [broo'-ho] witch (wizard)

camposanto [cam-po-san'-to] cemetery

con Díos [cone de'-os] with God (a blessing)

dame un besito [dah'-may oon bay-see'-to] give me a little kiss

de nada [day nah'-dah] it's nothing

descanso [des-cahn'-so] marker alongside a road, usually where somebody died

el Cristo Negro [el crees'-to nay'-gro] The Black Christ, the image of Christ with dark skin

estúpido [es-too'-pee-do] stupid person

felicidad [fay-le-see-dahd'] happiness

hijo de Díos [ee'-ho day de'-os] son of God

híjole [ee'-ho-lay] exclamation as in "Wow!" (slang)

hola [oh'lah] hello

huevos [oo-ay'-vos] balls, as in testicles (slang)

Indio [enn'de-o] Native American

Jesús Cristo [hay-soos' crees'-to] Jesus Christ

mariachi [mar-ey-ah'-chee] a type of music found in Mexico, lively and loud

mayordomo [mah-yor-do'-mo] village manager (usually of the acequia)

m'jito [mee-he'-to] my son (affectionate)

moco [mo'-co] snot; plural: *mocos* (slang)

mosca [mos'-cah] fly

muchacho [moo-chah'-cho] boy

muy bonita [moo'-e bo-nee'-ta] very pretty

muy importante [moo'-e im-por-tahn'-tay] very important

nada [nah'-dah] nothing

natillas [nah-tee'-yas] an egg pudding

nichos [nee'-chos] a nitch, hollowed in a wall, for placing decorations or religious items to make shrines

no hay problema [no ah'-ee pro-blay'-mah] it's not a problem

Our Lord of Esquípulas [es-key'-poo-las] In 1524 a Mayan chief named Esquípulas peacefully surrendered to the Spaniards. In his honor, the Spaniards named a new town for him in Guatemala. The crucifix at the Esquípulas Cathedral is carved of a dark wood, not unlike the color of the Mayan themselves, and is called *el Cristo Negro*. Both the crucifix and the earth surrounding the cathedral are believed by many to have curative powers. A cult grew around this church and this crucifix, inspiring pilgrimages. How the image of Our Lord of Esquípulas was transported to a New Mexico village with curative dirt remains a mystery—or a miracle.

pachuco [pah-cho'-co] a punk or a tough guy (slang)

padre [pah'-dray] Father, as in priest

pardóname [par-don'-a-may] pardon me

pendejo [pen-day'-ho] fool (slang)

penitentes [pay-ne-ten'-tay] members of a secret Catholic, religious order

perra [perr'-rah] female dog

perrita [per-ree'-ta] female puppy

pobrecito [po-bray-see'-to] poor little one

qué guapa [kay goo-ah'-pah] how beautiful, sexy, attractive

¿qué no? [kay no] why not?

refritos [ray-free'-tos] refried beans

señor [say-nyor'] sir

siétate [se-yet'-ta-tay] sit down

tortilla [tor-tee'-yah] flat, round, soft unleavened bread, made of corn or wheat

trastero [trahs-ter'-oh] a cabinet for clothes (also for dishes); plural: *trasteros*

un espectro [oon es-pec'-tro] a ghost

un peregrino [oon pay-ray-gree'-no] a pilgrim

vatos [va'-toes] guys, buddies

viejo [ve-ay'-ho] old man